Dracollus and The Ancient Clans

Book 1

The Bringer's Prophecy

Andrew Prescilla

For permission requests, write to the publisher, addressed "Attention: Permissions Coordinator" at the address below.

Lourdes Publishing
4000 W 106th St. Ste 125-411
Carmel, IN 46032

www.lourdespublishing.com

Book design © 2019
First printing

For information about special discounts for bulk purchases, sales promotions, fund-raising, and educational needs, please contact the publisher.

ISBN 978-1-948110-06-8

Printed in the United States of America

The Bringer's Prophecy

PROLOGUE

Life can have bad turns.
I had one of the worst on my seventeenth birthday.

Contents

Pronunciations

Allidan	(al-li-dan)
Brefalrus	(bre-fal-ruhs)
Bruday	(bru-dey)
Cselrane	(sel-reyn)
Curday	(kur-dey)
Dracollus	(dra-kol-loos)
Ezgamin	(ez-ga-min)
Gasepe	(ga-zip)
Haruasore	(ha-ru-a-sor)
Helmam	(hel-mam)
Helmamnor	(hel-mam-nor)
Hemirack	(he-mir-rak)
Housay	(hou-say)
Iptahvop	(ip-ta-vop)
Ilsa	(el-sa)
Jamano	(ja-mey-no)
Jarcannoph	(jar-can-nof)
Kaynory	(key-no-ree)
Linasslyc	(lin-as-slik)
Lunfa	(lun-fa)
Mairsday	(mairs-dey)
Mas Pal	(mas-pal)
Mriloslyc	(mi-ri-los-lik)
Mogirth	(moh-gurth)
Mutige	(mu-tic)
Phralorous	(fra-lo-ruhs)
Pireluve	(peer-loov)
Pluday	(ploo-dey)
Qahmicda	(kwa-mic-da)
Srmagon	(sur-ma-gon)
Sylfano	(sil-fa-no)
Thressday	(thres-dey)
Tlay	(ti-ley)
Ulpar	(ul-par)
Waldurrian	(wal-der-ree-an)
Xacunolyc	(eka-sa-koo-no-lik)
Zullyc	(zool-lik)

Chapter 1

A Totally Weird Day in School

I was feeling great when I woke up. It was the last day of school, and I would have the rest of my life to myself. You see, here in Housay, school officially ends after the eleventh grade. After that, one can do as one pleases - get a job, move into an apartment, or go to college. The only rule is that everyone who lives in Housay can only stay within the borders of Housay.

There are six districts in Housay. First, there's the Rich District where most of the affluent people live. This is the largest district and serves as the capital of Housay. Then there's the Middle District, which as the name suggests, is in the center of Housay and is where the middle-class people live. Most of the jobs are in The Working District, except for farming. The Industrial District is the area where transports, buses, trains, boats, and airplanes are manufactured. The Forest District is the wooded region where the wildlife lives. Nobody ventures to this place unless it's hunting season. Finally, there is the Farming District, which lives up to its name. There is no poor district in Housay. The Helmams, the natives of the planet Helmamnor, are generous people and there is opportunity for everyone.

The planet Helmamnor revolves around a blue sun Revfulcur, and there are seventeen planets in the Refular system. Helmamnor is the seventh planet in the system. Our skies are red and most of the plant leaves are yellow.

On Helmamnor, today is 17 16, 1717 ATWE. ATWE stands for After Truce Was Established. The truce that was established led to the creation of Housay. We have five light cycles: Curday, Thressday, Mairsday, Bruday, and Pluday. The time it takes for my planet to orbit Revfulcur is divided into 17 phases: Kaynory, Phralorous, Hemirack, Waldurrian, Iptahvop, Srmagon, Ezgamin, Tlay, Cselrane, Qahmicda, Ulpar, Brefalrus, Gasepe, Linasslyc, Xacunolyc, Mriloslyc, and Zullyc. These phases are named after those who have significantly contributed to the history of my planet. Five of the names belong to regular Helmams, while four of the names come from one superior race.

This strong and powerful race somewhat governs Housay, or so people say. This superior race is a very powerful race that lives in my world: Dragons. Dragons are all about power, strength, order, and peace. Dragons have kept an evil and ferocious race at by from our lands: Gargoyles. Gargoyles are very dangerous beings. They bring destruction and chaos. These creatures strike fear into anyone who sees them. Gargoyles basically look like giant bat-like creatures with a humanoid body. They would have ruled my world in fear if not for the stronger and more powerful Dragons that govern the Land of Housay. Gargoyles have been at bay from any conflict these last few hundreds of years. People say that if you were to see a dragon, you would be blessed with unimaginable power. However, not one dragon or gargoyle has ever been seen or heard of in Housay for the last eight hundred years. I myself don't think there was ever such a thing as a dragon or a gargoyle, and several people agree with me.

I live in the Middle District. The house where my parents and I live in is a simple Middle District house.

I got dressed for school and put on a plain red shirt and gray pants. I really wanted today to be over with; I was too excited that it was the day before my seventeenth birthday. I went downstairs and straight to the kitchen to eat mornfast, which is the first meal of the day. My mother was waiting for me and my father was cooking mornfast by the stove. The kitchen is made of a sink, a dishwasher that is right beside the sink, a rectangular island counter in the middle of the kitchen that is about thirteen krompus long and one krompus wide, a stove and oven by the door of the kitchen, a microwave above the stove and a refrigerator near the door. The kitchen walls are green with the floors dark brown. There were four gray metal chairs at the counter. My mother sat closest to the window.

"Good morning, Dracollus!" my mother Ilsa greeted.

"Morning, mom," I replied as I sat down.

"How are you feeling today?" my father Lunfa asked.

"Excited!" I exclaimed.

My father put bacon, eggs, and rice on my plate. This is my favorite mornfast! As soon as he put down my plate, I quickly devoured my mornfast. "Slow down, son!" my mother cautioned.

"I'm sorry, mom," I said, not taking a break from eating my mornfast. "I have to meet up with Jamano and Haruasore before I go to school."

Haruasore and Jamano have been my best friends for as long as I can remember. When we were kids, I would always joke with them, saying that they would look cute together. They would constantly tell me to knock it off. They finally started dating last year. When they told me that they were dating, I told them that I was fine with it. I already had my eyes on another girl. Besides, I've always thought of Jamano as my sister and considered Haruasore as my best friend. They seemed like the perfect couple. I was really happy for them.

"Well, don't worry," my father reminded me. "School doesn't start until 8 o'clock, and it's only 7:30."

"I know dad. I just want to ask them if they were doing anything special for me on my birthday."

When I said this, my parents had a worried look on their faces.

"Well," my mother said, "your father and I think that you should celebrate your birthday with just the two of us."

"What?" My eyes widened in bewilderment.

"Just this time. We have something very special for you."

"What is it?" I asked inquisitively.

"It's something very special, and we want it to be a surprise," my father said.

"Ok. I should get going. I don't want to miss talking to my friends before I finish school."

I then left my house and walked the three blocks to Gray Wall, my high school, which is a 17-minute walk. There is nothing special about my walk; just go down a couple of streets and then I arrive at my school, Gray Wall.

When I got there, I went to the back of the school, where I usually meet Jamano and Haruasore. The back of the school is a small field of grass, which is where most students like to hang out. If you are facing the school, the parking lot is on the right side and the track field is on the left side. Gray Wall High School has four buildings, one each for building; math, science, literature, and sports. The buildings aren't very big, nor tall. Each building has two floors and about 34 rooms, with the exception of the sports building which only has one floor with 16 rooms and a dome at the end of the building. The literature building is the main building of the school. It is where the cafeteria is located, as well as the principal's office and vice principal's office. Our rooms have windows in each room and a rectangular window on all the doors. I went to my friends and I saw that they were holding hands.

"Hey!" they greeted me.

"Happy Early Birthday!" Haruasore said.

"Haruasore! I told you to wish me 'Happy Birthday' tomorrow!"

"I know, but Jamano and I have a really cool plan for you tomorrow, and I just got so excited I could hardly keep it."

"Besides," he said sounding all serious now, "we have been planning it for weeks, so you should at least give me an apology for me trying to hold back my excitement. If you knew how long Jamano has been talking nonstop about what we're planning, you would know I have to blow off some of my excitement!"

That's one thing with Haruasore. He can be so serious one minute, the next he's goofing around and vice versa. If he wasn't so serious, I'd say he was one of those jerks in school. He's very muscular, tall, has brown eyes, and has cool features on his face such as sharp eyes and well-defined jaw muscles. That's what I'd think jerks are like at. Jamano, on the other hand, is sweet, kind, short and nerdy. She can memorize anything she sees. She talks about everything but knows when to keep quiet. She also has this look in her sky blue eyes that make you feel warm and comforted. I guess that's why they seem to like each other. Haruasore is everything Jamano is not, and Jamano is everything Haruasore is not. Do opposites attract?

"Yeah, 'bout that." I said, "My parents want me to spend my birthday with them only."

"What?!" they replied, visibly shocked physically and in unison.

"That is not like them." Jamano blurted.

"They said they have a special surprise for me, but they never said what it was."

"What do you think it is Dracollus?" Haruasore asked.

"I don't-"

"Excuse me, Dracollus," a voice interrupted.

I turned to see that it was Sylfano from my History class. She's the kind of girl that likes to be alone. She doesn't hang out with anyone, but she always participates in class. I guess that's because she lives with her uncle, who's kind of strict. She doesn't talk about what happened to her parents; then again, she doesn't talk to anyone unless it's part of the class activity. I have a confession to make, I've had a huge crush on her since I met her when I was 14. I mean who wouldn't like her? She has straight red hair that reaches her shoulders, green eyes that look almost reptilian, tan colored skin, a beautiful smile, straight white teeth, about average in height for a girl about, very beautiful, and… well, you get the idea of why I like her. Anyway, I was surprised she spoke to me.

"Uh, Hi Sylfano," I said dumbly.

"Hi, I couldn't help myself hearing that it will be your birthday tomorrow," she declared.

"Uh, yeah that's right."

"So listen Dracollus, I was wondering if I could ask you to come to dinner at *The Red Dragon's Lair* tonight?"

I was completely speechless at this point, so I tried to sound smart by saying "Um, well, I…"

"Dracollus," Sylfano said with a smile. "What's happening here is that I'm asking you on a date. That is if you're not doing anything with your friends here."

I was so flabbergasted to her proposal. My mind was completely blank. I was dazed for a few minutes, so when I could think clearly again I heard Jamano had said to her "No, Dracollus is completely free tonight. He'd love to go to dinner with you. He'll see you at the restaurant at 8:30."

"Great! I'll see you in class later, Dracollus."

Sylfano turned and left toward the school. I faced Jamano and yelled, "What did you do?"

"I got you a date with the girl you have been drooling over since the 9th grade." Jamano replied, "You should thank me!"

"What am I going to tell my parents? You know they already have plans for me, and they don't like me anywhere near Sylfano."

"Well, you could tell them what you'll be doing tonight, or you could pretend to go to bed at 8 o'clock and use pillows to sneak out of your room."

"I've never snuck out of the house before!"

"Well, there's a first time for everything." Haruasore said, "Like your hot date tonight! You should be more excited or nervous that you are about to go on a date with the girl of your dreams, or maybe you could tell your parents that you're celebrating your birthday with Jamano and me, but really you have a hot date."

"Cut it out, man!" I said. "I'm sweating like crazy now, and you're not helping me at all!"

"Well," Haruasore said "Excuse me, but I'm not the one who got all speechless when Sylfano asked you on a date. Hey! That gives me an idea."

"What is it?" Jamano inquired.

"What if we go with Dracollus to *The Red Dragon's Lair*, like a double date?"

"Haruasore!" I said, "That is one of your worst ideas ever. Knowing you, you'd probably make me look like a fool in front of Sylfano. I know you wouldn't do it on purpose, or in front of Jamano, but you can't resist the goofy habits you have."

"Dracollus is right" Jamano replied, "You have matured over the past few months, but occasionally you still make fun of me when we're out on a date, and when I say make fun of me, I mean it in a bad way. Take that time when we were at that school play - we were watching the performers and in the end, you went up on stage and rapped an inappropriate song about me."

Haruasore thought about it for a while. "I guess you guys are right," Haruasore admitted.

"Wait a minute!" I said. "Was this part of your plan for my birthday? Was being on a date with Sylfano the way you were going to celebrate my birthday?"

"What? No!" Jamano said, "I mean, this date with Sylfano is awesome, but I could never get Sylfano to talk."

"And I for one cannot believe that you can think like that after that little speech Jamano gave about me on being a fool on a date," Haruasore said. "I'm offended."

I felt a little embarrassed by this outburst. "Well, sorry man. I didn't mean to offend you. I apologize."

Just then the bell rang. We'd been so focused on the date with Sylfano, we lost track of time. "I'll see you guys in Geology!" I yelled as I headed off to my first class.

■ ■

My morning classes were mostly boring, much like how you would expect the last day of school to be, except for my history class. Since it was the last day of class the teacher just played some music videos on the computer. My class got to listen to all kinds of music favorites today. Normally the teacher would only let us listen to Woox music, but I guess since it was the last day of school the teacher was trying to be nice. The room was organized in rows of five and there were twenty-five students in the class. The desk was a complete circle facing the front of the room with our back against the door. In front of us were a giant whiteboard and an overhead projector above it. That is how my class watched the music videos. During this really cool music video, I felt that someone was staring at me. When I turned to look, I found that it was Sylfano. The moment we made eye contact she smiled and waved at me. I was a little happy and a little confused by this. I kept wondering what I was going to tell her on our date, and I just went into a daze. Class ended before I could even consider what I was going to do. When the bell rang I left for the cafeteria for lunch. I got bread, smoked pork, peeled carrots, and raw apple slices. The cafeteria is huge. It is able to hold about seventy students at a time with thirty tables that we can move around. The tables are about twenty krompus long and a krompus wide. I don't have the same lunch time as Haruasore and Jamano, so I couldn't talk to them. I sat with some other people that were in my science class. Some cycles, I have the same lunch time as Sylfano; today would happen to be one of those cycles. Normally, she would be sitting at a table in a corner all by herself, but today, she wasn't there. With eight minutes of lunch left, I started to wonder what was going on with her. She suddenly appeared next to me.

"Come and sit with me at my table," Sylfano requested.

Again, I was rendered speechless by this sudden approach, so I said the best thing I could think of. "But there's only 8 minutes until lunch is over."

"Come on," she said reassuringly, "this will only take 5 minutes!"

Feeling like I had no choice, I decided to play along. I took what was left of my lunch, threw it in the trash and let Sylfano lead the way to her table. I was very aware that as we walked to Sylfano's little corner table, a lot of eyes focused on. One of those sets of eyes was Pireluve. Pireluve is about average in height, has pale skin, shaggy short black hair, and gray eyes. I have a rocky past with him, but later on, we would be enemies in the end. I'll tell you more about later. Anyway, moving on, I heard that a lot of people think Sylfano is very pretty, but when people ask her out she declines. Other times she just ignores people, as she does in class. As far as I can tell she's not very social with anyone. She sat in the corner, while I pulled up a chair and sat across from her. There was a great deal of silence. After about a few minutes of silence, I decided to break the ice by saying, "So what is it you wanted to talk about?"

"Well," Sylfano replied, "I just wanted to tell you about this whole date."

"Ok," I said dumbly.

"No, I'm not dropping it now, if that's what you were thinking about. It's just," She paused for a second. "I've liked you since tenth grade, but I was always too shy to ask you out." I was even more shocked by this revelation. "Besides, my uncle doesn't like me to hang out with people."

"I know that your uncle is strict, but doesn't he allow you to have any of fun?" I inquired.

"Well, he does allow me to do things which I consider fun, which you wouldn't consider fun."

"What happened to your parents? You never bring that up when there are questions in class about family members." Sylfano was quiet for a long time. Finally, she said "Both of my parents did some really bad things in the past. Because of their past, I came here to Housay for safety." I realized that I was way over my head with this conversation.

"You mean you've lived in a place outside the borders?" I asked with increasing amazement.

"Yes," she said, "You wouldn't believe how dangerous it is outside the borderline. My uncle and I had to sneak inside. We have lived in some peaceful manners afterward making sure the law would not find us."

"Is that why your uncle is so strict?" I asked.

"That's one of the main reasons. But there are other reasons why he's so strict." She put her hand on my hand. Now they say a special feeling occurs when someone that is special to you touches you. Well, when she touched me I felt nervous, happy, and worried. However, these weren't my feelings they were coming from Sylfano. I viscously took my hand away from her hand. "What's wrong?" She asked, shocked.

I didn't know what to say. "Nothing," I said. "It's… It's just I was completely surprised by your sudden approach like that." Just then the bell rang signaling that lunch was over.

"I better be off to my next class, Sylfano." I hurried to my Science of the Land class, with Haruasore and Jamano.

When I got to the room, they were already waiting for me. "Hey!" they said in unison.
"Hey," I replied back. "How was your last day of lunch here?" Jamano asked me.

"It was…gr- gr- great," I stammered.

"Did something happen to you, man?" Haruasore asked curiously. "'There's a hint of softness when something…"

"I'll tell you later when we get the chance," I said a little nervous now. How was I going to tell them about the touching-and-feeling-Sylfano's-emotion episode? I usually share all my secrets with them, but now I'm just flabbergasted. We sat in a row of nine seats and filled in three. The bell rang, and the teacher said we could do whatever we wanted to do, just as long as we keep it quiet because the class next door was watching a movie.

"Sooooooo…" Jamano started off.

"What happened at lunch?" Haruasore asked again.

"Well," I started, "Sylfano made me sit with her at her table today." Jamano looked shocked, but Haruasore just sighed.

"THAT is what the big deal was all about?" he said, sounding like he was annoyed. "You have a date with her tonight, with no idea what you're going to wear, and not sure what it is she likes to eat, and you're worried about a little conversation that happened for only 8 minutes."

"How did you know that the conversation was only 8 minutes long?" I asked suspiciously.

"Well, here's the thing," he said, "When I was in the middle of my Art class, she came in and asked the teacher something. I don't what it was but it took like 17 minutes of the class time, I put the time together and that left her with about 10 minutes of lunch, give or take."

"Since when could you do math?" Jamano asked, "I always thought you were more of a history and self-defense kind of studying kind of guy."

"I always told you guys I needed to stay after school to get extra help with math class and science work. I can't believe you never believe me."

"Oh, no." I said, "We do believe. It's just that we never actually believed that you would spend all that time with extra help."

"Well," Haruasore replied with a huge grin on his face, "I do spend most of the time after school for extra help, but like you said I don't spend ALL after school doing extra help." We all laughed at this. In his spare time Haruasore likes to practice martial arts and if he practices here in the school, he makes a complete fool of himself.

"That sounds like the Haruasore we all know," I said.

"Did you ever doubt what I do after school?" Haruasore asked. He then gave me a slap on the back.

When he slapped me, I got the exact thing feeling of what happened with Sylfano. Only this time I got the feelings of happiness, excitement, and goofiness. It also came very fast and abruptly that I almost fell forward on the desk, but I caught myself.

"Dracollus!" Jamano said worriedly, "What's wrong?" It took me a couple of minutes to recover, and by then I realized that my face was covered in sweat. "It happened again!" I replied sounding exhausted.

"What happened again?" Haruasore asked me.

"Well," I replied with a shaggy breath. "When I was at the cafeteria with Sylfano, she put her hand on my hand."

"Oh, don't tell me you almost passed out from that." Haruasore said, "I mean, you can get all emotional from the-"

"But that's the thing!" I said abruptly, "It was all emotional. I was feeling things I shouldn't have been able to feel."

"That's normal," Jamano said, "I felt a whole bunch of emotions that I didn't expect to feel the first time Haruasore and I held hands for the first time."

"Well, did you get to know exactly how she was feeling when you touched her?" I asked curiously, "Because that's what I felt when Sylfano touched me."

Haruasore then asked, "What do you mean exactly? Can you explain it better?"

"Well," I tried to think of a better way to explain it in better detail. "I know that you're all curious about this. I get that, but when I touch you right now like this," I touched his arm and I felt curiosity coming from him. "I can actually feel that you are curious. It's not my feelings that I get when I touch you, they are yours. I can tell that they are yours because I am experiencing my own feelings as well. I can tell the difference between my feelings and your feelings. Your emotions feel like they are invading my emotions." I then took my hand off his arm. Haruasore and I looked at Jamano for some answer.

Jamano was very quiet for a good five minutes. "That's a really interesting feeling that you're sensing!" she finally said.

"Do you know what's happening to me?" I asked, "I mean I know you're not a doctor, but do you know what it means?"

"Well from the sound of it, it looks as if your emotional state is making you experience not just your feeling, but much more – those of the people you are having physical contact with. Either that or, and this is my best guess, you have some kind of transpathy that's more developed than the rest of us."

"Now hold it right there. You're not saying that I'm going to become some kind of psychic, like what you've become now, are you?" I was more intrigued than ever.

Jamano always had a thing about knowing things better than anyone. About six weeks ago she developed a thing that makes her know what will happen before it even happens. For example, we had to take the final exams two cycles ago, and Jamano had guessed the results of the exams. When we got them back, every score was just as she said they would be. She even predicted what the other students' in a different class she had scores would be, and she got it right 100%. However, she's not the only one who is like a psychic in her family. Jamano's father is a very famous hypnotist, her mother is a fortuneteller, her older brother is a magician/illusionist, and her little sister is a girl obsessed with studying sorcery. Jamano has tried to fit in with society, but coming from a family like this makes it very difficult to do that.

"I'm not saying that you're going to become like me." Jamano says, "I'm saying that this could be something that's happening to you because of your current emotional state. This could make you feel more of other people's emotions than your own."

"That really makes no sense to me whatsoever," I said.

"Well, maybe you could understand it better if you held my hand with your hand," she offered, extending her hand.

I was kind of nervous with this gesture, as I did not want to be part of Jamano's inner world. I thought about it for a good long minute before I finally extended my hand and took Jamano's hand with mine. The moment I touched her, a cacophony of feelings came upon me. It was a stream of curiosity, confusion, and excitement. I knew instantly that those feelings were emanating from Jamano. She was quiet for a minute, then I noticed that her eyes were turning glassy. After about a minute she screamed and let my hand go. Her screaming was so loud that my ears popped. Everyone in the class was looking at us. It was until then that I realized Jamano's hand was on fire! I was so shocked that the only thing I could do was look at my right hand. There was smoke coming off them, but there didn't seem to be any burn marks. Jamano's hand was still on fire when the teacher finally noticed.

"Help!" Jamano yelled.

"Somebody put the fire out of Jamano's hand while I call the healer!" the teacher yelled.

Haruasore opened his bottle of water and splashed all of its contents on Jamano's hand. The fire was out instantly, but Jamano was still screaming.

Haruasore then hugged her and tried to calm her down as best he could.

"It's going to be OK," he said to her reassuringly, "Everything is going to be just fine…"

Jamano lowered her screaming. My ears were no longer ringing. I was still in shock, but I found the courage to ask, "What happened, Jamano? How did your hand catch fire?"

Jamano finally stopped screaming and started to cry.

"Hey," I told her reassuringly as best I could, "The fire is out, and there is nothing to worry about anymore."

Jamano just looked me in the eyes with her sky blue eyes and told me "I saw a lot of fire in your future Dracollus, as well as some lies about your past that will change you."

I looked at her confusedly.

She continued, "There was also a lot of stone, and some kind of strange birds in your future."

Before she could tell me more, the teacher from class for next door came to the door. He asked our teacher what and she told him what happened. The healer then arrived. Jamano went to the healer's office for some medicine for her hand. Haruasore joined her at the healer's office, telling the healer that he could calm her down a bit further as needed.

The rest of the school day was a blur. I don't know what exactly happened to Jamano after school ended. She wasn't at the healer's office when I got there at the end of school. I asked the healer what happened to her, and he told me that she had to be dismissed early for some rest and to recover. As for Haruasore, he had to go back to class after Jamano got her bandage. According to him, she had received second-degree burns all over her hand. The healer said she would have to have it wrapped in bandages for a few cycles, but she could still use it afterward.

"She is very lucky." The healer said, "A few more seconds and the damage to her hand would have been severe."

The healer then asked me what exactly happened to Jamano. I told him that we were holding hands when all of a sudden her hand caught fire. He was a little skeptical when I told him this, but he stated that Jamano and Haruasore told him the exact same story earlier.

I decided that I should visit Jamano. When I got to her house she answered the door, but she told me to go home and be ready for my date. I was a little confused by this because it was only 2:30 right now, and I was supposed to be at The Red Dragon's Lair at 8:30. She also told me, "You have to go tell your parents about your plans for tonight, but you should bend the truth a little."

I thought about it. "I guess…" I started to say.

"Great!" Jamano said eagerly. "So you tell your parents about how you're celebrating your birthday when you get home. And oh, yeah," She said surprisingly as if she forgot something.

"Can you do me a favor?" she asked.

I replied, "Of course I would. Anything to help you feel better."

"Don't tell your parents about this little incident that happened to me. I don't want them ruining your hot date on your birthday."

"Jamano," I told her, "I wasn't even planning on telling them anything about what happened to you today."

"You weren't?" she asked surprised.

"I mean come on, who's going to believe all this stuff that is happening to me aside from you? Even I still don't understand what's going on with me, and I bet you don't either. That reminds me, what did you see in your little psychic vision anyway?" I asked teasingly.

Jamano looked very scared and worried when I brought this up.

"You better go back home, Dracollus. Like you said before, I am still unsure about what's going on with you."

"But you do have some kind of idea though, right?"

"Just go home, Dracollus," she said, and then closed the door. I was still a little confused, but I opted to go home.

Chapter 2

An Unforgettable Date On My Birthday

It took me about half an hour, to walk from Jamano's to my house. I was very surprised when I realized how fast it took me to get home; it usually took me about an hour of walking. I didn't even take the shortcut through the school, which would save me about seven minutes had I taken it. I guess with all the weird stuff happening today, I might have just wanted to cool down before my date tonight.

I arrived home earlier than expected.

"Welcome home!" my father greeted me from the living room.

"How was your last day of school?" my mother asked excitedly.

"Everything was great today." I lied.

My mother then asked me, "Well, what about the little chat with your friends this morning. Did you tell them that you were spending your birthday with us?"

"Yeah," I said, "they didn't seem too happy when I told them, but they decided to celebrate it tonight with me." I was a little worried if they were going to buy this story.

"Oh, really," my father said surprised, "where are you going and at what time?"

"We're going to *The Red Dragon's Lair* for dinner to celebrate my birthday. I'll meet the guys at 8:25."

My parents then faced each other with weird looks on their faces. "Isn't that the closest restaurant to where Sylfano lives?" my father asked. I was nervous by then, thinking they were going to find out about my little white lie.

"Yeah," I replied, "But I don't think that really matters at the moment."

"Of course not," my mother told me. "We just want to make sure that you're in good hands and at a good place for your birthday."

"Why would you think that…Oh, you mean her uncle?"

"That right," my father said, "you should try and avoid him as best as you can."

"Well, I was never even going anywhere near him or his niece," I continued to lie. "So may I go?"

"Of course you may," my mother said, "just stay far away from those two as possible."

"I'll do my best with Sylfano's uncle." I proceeded to my room before they figured out the deception within my little sentence. I decided that I should call my friends to meet me at *The Red Dragon's Lair* just in case my parents decided to check up on me during my date.

Time continued to fly very fast. A moment ago, I was in my room and it was only 3:10 pm., the next it was 7:45 pm. I don't remember exactly what happened to me in those four hours. The last thing I remember was receiving a text from Haruasore saying he would meet me there, but Jamano had to stay home due to her injuries. At 7:46, I took a shower and got dressed a little fancy for my date night. I was wearing my favorite white collared shirt with a dark blue, almost black, suit and jacket with a pair of pants matching. I wore dress socks and dress shoes. By the time I finished dressing it was 8:15. My parents offered to drive me, but I told them that I wanted to drive myself to the restaurant. They simply smiled and let me know that I should be home by ten. I left the house and entered the family transport. "Have a good time at your birthday night!" my parents said. I waved to them and drove to the restaurant.

I arrived at the restaurant within fourteen minutes, which meant I was a minute early. I parked my transport at the restaurant's parking lot and then went to the entrance of the restaurant where Haruasore was waiting.

"Do you want me to come with you to the restaurant?" he asked.

"Yeah," I replied, "but only for a few minutes. I don't want her to feel weird."

We entered the restaurant and saw Sylfano at the closest table nearest the hostess. She was absolutely stunning wearing a sapphire dress, diamond earrings, a silver bracelet, and a golden link necklace. The rest of the place was almost as amazing as Sylfano. The walls were blue and the ceiling was green with red dragons all over the ceiling. There was a buffet section at the back of the restaurant, which was full of guests, but since Sylfano sat closet to the front of the restaurant, I got the impression that she didn't want to have a buffet. There were paper lanterns hanging from the walls, and there were servers who all looked the same. They had slanted dark brown eyes, short straight black hair for the men, long straight brown hair for the women and tan-colored skin. The tables were brown, covered with black cloths and the napkins were red. The chairs were beige and the seats had a red cushion. Haruasore whistled. "That is one smoking hot date you have," Haruasore whispered.

"Yeah, uh why don't you leave now man? I don't think my parents are spying on me anymore."

"OK. See you later," he said as he left.

I went to sit across from Sylfano. She smiled as I sat down. "I'm glad you made it."

"I'm glad you're here with me to celebrate my birthday," I said.

"Well, what about your friends? I thought they were coming too?"

"Uh, yeah about that-" I was cut short by the severer, who arrived with some water and menus. As soon as he left I told Sylfano that Jamano had other plans. "How's her hand, by the way?" she inquired.

"How do you know about that?" I asked curiously.

"I overheard someone from your class talk about it. Is that why she isn't here now?"

"Yeah," I replied, "Jamano couldn't come and Haruasore wanted to be with her, but he wanted to see how you looked like tonight. Besides, he would have embarrassed me in front of you, so I'm fine with this arrangement."

"Well, what about you, why wasn't your hand burned?"

"What are you talking about?"

"Well..." She said with a little hesitation, "From what I heard you were holding hands with her when her hand caught fire. So why wasn't your hand burned?"

At this point, I somehow got the impression that Sylfano was hiding something from me. I decided to play along with her, so I said, "I don't know, but I am glad that Jamano is fine now."

"Oh well, as long as you're happy, I'm happy."

I then put my hand on her hand. I immediately felt her emotions again. She was feeling nervous, scared and worried. I was going to have to get used to this strange thing that's happening to me. We talked while we ordered and while we ate. I had something called Commander's Bird and fried brown rice while Sylfano had soup noodles. The noodles were white, flat, and short. I have never seen these kinds of noodles before.

I got to understand Sylfano a little bit more. She still wouldn't talk much about her past, especially what it was like outside the Housay or her parents. She did tell me that she sometimes talks to her father but not her mother. According to Sylfano, her mother has a very important job that takes up a lot of time. That's why she doesn't have time to chat with her daughter. I was a little saddened by this news. She won't talk any more about her past or her family, but I did find out more about Sylfano in general. It turns out that Sylfano's favorite color is silver, that she also lives in the rich district and is a huge fan of mythology, just like me. We had a very delicious dinner with fortune cookies for dessert.

When I opened my cookie, I was a little scared about what the paper said. "What does yours say?" Sylfano asked me.

"Your life will change when you find out the truth."

Sylfano looked very scared when I finished the sentence. "I'm sure it's nothing. I mean mine says 'The past is the key to your future.' That could mean anything."

"I guess," I said as I reached out towards her and put my hand on her shoulder. I instantly felt the urge to run away. At least, that is what I was feeling from Sylfano. "Why don't I drop you off at your house?"

"That's a great idea," she said excitedly, "since I actually walked here."

"You walked?" I asked very curiously. From my understanding of what Sylfano told me, her house was at least 34 dlaus away from here.

"I'm sorry," she said apologetically, "I meant to say I took a bus and walked a block."

"Oh, that makes sense now. Let me pay for dinner."

"Oh no, let me do that," she offered.

"I think I should do that. I'm the gentleman here."

"Yes, but I was the one who asked you to on a date." She paid for our meal using blue emeralds (our currency at Housay). I then walked her to the transport and opened the door for her. Afterward, I got in the transport and started driving. Sylfano gave me directions to her home. It took us about 71 minutes to drive to her house, thanks to a lot of traffic near the border of the Middle and Rich District. When we got to her house, I was amazed at how big her house was and that it was in the middle of appears to be the only meadow of the Rich District. The meadow led to a forest at the backyard. I've never been to the Rich District before, so I wouldn't know if it actually does lead to the forest district. I got out of the transport first, and then I opened the door for Sylfano.

"Thanks for the ride."

"Anytime," I replied, "Actually, I forgot to ask you something at the restaurant."

"What's that?" she asked with a hint of nervousness in her voice.

"Why do you go to a high school in the middle district, like the <u>Gray Wall</u>, instead of going to a high school here in the Rich District, like the <u>Blue Skies</u>?" I inquired.

Sylfano giggled at this question. "I'll tell you on our next date." She then kissed me on the lips.

Now, after all, that has happened to me today, I would think that a kiss should have no effect on me. Well, I was wrong! About two seconds into the kiss, my mind was filled with images I couldn't make out; a blue dragon with a golden crown on its head, a palace from an ancient kingdom being buried under a mountain range of green soil and yellow plants, a gold dragon changing into a man, and a scroll with what appears to be some kind of prophecy on it. I quickly broke away from Sylfano.

"Dracollus," she said, "What's wrong? You look like you've just seen a ghost."

I had to think of a good excuse for why I was looking at her strangely, so I said the kind of obvious thing about the sudden kiss, "Nothing… I just didn't expect you to do that."

"You didn't like it?" she asked sadly.

"NO! I mean… I didn't think that after our first date you would do that." I started to feel a little sick after I said this.

"I should go now," I whispered as I got into my transport.

"Dracollus, are you ok?" Sylfano asked, sounding concerned.

"**Yeah I'm fine,**" I said. The way I said it, didn't sound like the native language Jarcannoph but a different language. I drove off a little quickly. On the way home I started to burn up quickly. The AC was on at full blast, but I was still sweating like crazy. My lungs were starting to feel tight, and I felt like throwing up. I got to my house after 85 minutes, still feeling like this. By then I was breathing a little hard. I turned off the transport and went inside my house. The lights were off, so I assumed my parents were asleep. I went upstairs to my room and quickly got changed. I removed all my dress clothes and only wore my underwear and fell asleep as soon as I fell on my bed.

That night, I had the weirdest dream ever. They were two dreams that merged into one. The first dream was about Sylfano. I saw her in what I assumed was her house, and she was pacing back and forth looking very serious. Interestingly she was still wearing the dress she wore for our date.

"How was the date?" a voice said to her, as a man emerged from the shadows.

"The date went well," she said to the man, "but things got a little difficult at the end of the night."

"How so?" the man asked her. Looking at him more closely, I realized that I had never seen him before. This man was not her uncle. He had black hair, almost reptilian green eyes, tan-colored skin, and was wearing a gold crown on his head.

"It looks like he is not a regular Helmam," she declared.

"What do you mean?" the man asked impatiently.

"He read my mind before he left, and he felt my emotions when he touched me. It seems like he's one of us. He spoke in the ancient language of the Dragon."

"There is another possibility," A man said as he came into the picture. He had a blue Shirt on and was wearing dress pants. He had a mustache and a long brown beard. His eyes were so dark that they looked like they had no pupils in them. When I looked at him, I recognized him as Sylfano's uncle, Jacob Mas Pal.

"This boy could have inherited these powers from his parents," Jacob Mas Pal continued, "they could have also taught him the language if they have studied the magic of Dragons."

"Well, something is definitely not right about the situation," Sylfano said. "And I don't need your insights about this, Jacob - after all you are only my guardian."

"Calm down, my daughter," said the other man, "I'm sure whatever is going on, Lunfa and Ilsa will talk eventually when you confront them." At this point, I was completely confused about what was going on.

"We can't," said Jacob, "we have no idea where they are going for Dracollus' birthday."

"I may have an idea," Sylfano said with a smile.

■■

That's when my dream changed. In this second dream, I was in a room full of fire! I could feel all the heat from the room coming to me. Except nothing was burning. There was something across the room, which at first I could not make out. I walked a little closer and saw that it was a dragon. When the dragon saw me it pointed a finger (or was it a claw?) at me and said with a loud voice in another language, "*__Fulfill your destiny. You are the only one that can right my wrongs, and save this world.__*"

That's when I woke up. My father was standing beside my bed.

"Hey son, I was just about to wake you up and wish you a happy birthday," he said.

"Uh yeah, thanks dad," I replied sleepily.

"So how did last night go?"

"Uh, last night was…" I didn't know what to say. "Last night was very interesting."

"Well, today is going to be even more interesting," he said this with a smile, but he had this strange look in his eyes. It was as if he was feeling bad about something.

"To start the day, here's your present from me." He handed me a little box that was tied by a piece of string. I untied the string and opened the box. Inside the box, there was a necklace with a pendant on it. The pendant was blue and it looked like a snake. On the snake, there were some designs that I thought were awesome.

"Cool! Thanks, dad!"

"You're welcome, son. Now get dressed and come downstairs, there's mornfast waiting for you."

I put on a new set of clothes, black shorts, yellow Shirt, and the necklace. When I saw it in my reflection, it looked pretty good on me. I went downstairs to the kitchen. On the table were bacon, pancakes, and waffles.

"Happy birthday, Dracollus!" my mother greeted.

"Thanks, mom!"

I filled my plate with waffles and bacon first before I ate some pancakes. We all ate silently and very slowly. When we were all done I collected all the dishes and pans and decided to wash all them.

"Dracollus, since when do you like washing the dishes?" my mother asked me.

"I don't really know," I confessed, "I just felt like it." Mornfast was really quiet and I don't know what's happening today. I thought that doing something

I hated would help calm me down. Instead of feeling comfort I started to sense guilt, sadness, and anxiety coming from my parents. I couldn't see their expressions with my back to them.

"Well, we are going somewhere special for your birthday," my mother continued, "It's going to be a long drive, but it will be worth it."

"Ok," I said dumbly, "When are we leaving?"

"We can leave as soon as I get some things," my father replied. "You can go to the transport now."

"Alright." When I got to the transport I sat in the back seat, while my mother got in the driver's seat. We waited in silence for a few minutes, and then my father got into the passenger's seat. Now that we were all together, we started our long drive.

We drove for about 5 hours before we finally stopped. "We're here," my father finally said.

We all got out of the transport and I looked at the place where we had arrived. We were parked in front of what appeared to be an old temple. I knew immediately that we were in the Ancient District. The Ancient District is made of two different areas: the Forbidden Area and the Historical Area. Not many people are allowed in this place (which is why I never mentioned it before), so I was wondering why we were here. I was also curious as to what area I was in. From what I understand the Historical Area is where all records of Housay are kept. As for the Forbidden Area, I have no idea what goes on in there. I was also wondering how my parents could get us in this place. As far as I knew they had never mentioned anything about the Ancient District in my entire life.

"Where are we?" I asked

"You don't recognize this place?" my father quizzed me.

"No, I don't."

"You visited this place when you were just a baby. You haven't been here since."

"So why are we here?"

Before I could get an answer, a voice came from behind me saying my name. I turned around to see Sylfano and her uncle standing in front of another building. They came towards us, not looking very happy.

"What are you two doing here?" my mother asked angrily.

"We are here because we want to ask you some more questions about Dracollus," Jacob Mas Pal retorted.

"Not today, it's his birthday. Besides you can't make us tell you anything."

"We have a right to know with who he is. He could be a danger to us and to our people."

"You and Sylfano are only here because this is a safe place from the war," my father said, "You can't expect us to help you by answering all your questions about what we do."

At this point, I started to get nervous and a little scared. I stepped in between my parents and Sylfano and her uncle.

"Hey," I said trying to break up this argument, "Can we stop this, please. I don't know what you guys are talking about, but you're all-"

That's when I started to feel sore. A sudden shot of pain came up out of nowhere. I crumpled to my knees, hugged my stomach, and shut my eyes. I groaned in pain.

"Dracollus," my father said, "What's wrong?"

I groaned before I responded. "Oh! My insides feel like they're on fire." I moaned. I continued to moan, but soon after my moaning started to sound like a growl.

"Oh, no," My father exclaimed as he got on to his knees. "Dracollus, look at me!" I opened my eyes to see he looked worried. "Focus on me, and remember who you are."

I looked a little to the left to see a clock on the wall of the temple. The clock was about 50 krompus away from me, but I could still read the time. The clock showed that it was past 17 o'clock 17 minutes and 11 seconds. My vision had become red, and I meanly looked at my father and said in another language, "***I know exactly who I am, and I will fulfill my destiny,***" and then my vision became orange…

Chapter 3

The Revelation

I woke up with a start, sat upright and gasped for air.

"Dracollus!" I heard two voices say in unison. "Are you alright?"

I looked around me, and I realized that I was in my own bedroom, and the voices came from my parents, who were sitting by the bedside. Before I could recall what had happened for me to end up here I, realized that it was dark in my room. I looked at my clock and I soon found out why it was so dark in my room, it was fifteen o'clock at night.

"Why are we in the dark?" I asked.

"It was a necessary thing to do after what happened earlier today," my mother replied.

"Yeah," I started off, "about that. What exactly happened today, mom?"

Someone finally turned on the lights. I got a better look at my parents now. They were all covered in soot, and they had cuts and bruises all over their arms and bodies. My mother's usually neat long black hair was cut short, so it was no longer far below her shoulders, but only reached her ears and it was messy as if she had just come out of bed. There was also a red substance in her hair, which I assumed that was blood. Her right blue eye was closed while her left green eye was open. My father was in worse shape. His blond hair was a rat's nest when he always kept it straight and neat. He had so much soot in his hair that it almost looked black. His brown eyes were bloodshot.

"What do you remember, Dracollus?" my father pressed.

"Not much," I replied dumbly. "I remember that we were in front of this temple at the Ancient District, you guys arguing with Sylfano and her uncle, and this pain inside me. That's pretty much it."

"Can you remember anything after that?" my mother asked.

"No, why? What happened?"

My mother turned on the monitor in my room. On the screen was a news reporter standing in front of what appeared to be the Ancient District. Only, the place was wrecked and on fire. There were some people trying to put out the flames, but I was more focused on the reporter.

"-still unsure about what exactly happened here in the Ancient District, but some witnesses claim that there was a dragon in the sky that was breathing fire throughout the place," the reporter said. "According to some of them, the dragon was apparently flying in circles as if it were confused. None of the witnesses, however…" She stopped talking for a second and put one of her fingers to her left ear. I knew immediately that she was receiving new information from her news station. After a few more seconds of silence, her face lit up.

"Wait. This just came in!" she said. "One of the witnesses made a video of what happened. We now bring you the following footage."

The screen changed to a different video. This video showed a golden dragon in the sky flying and breathing fire. The dragon looked angry but confused. I could tell it was confused because it was flying in circles and then went flying in zigzags. Before I could find out any more information, my mother turned off the monitor.

"That's what happened, Dracollus," she said sadly.

"Wait, how exactly did we-"

"Dracollus," My father cut me off. "I think it's about time you learn the truth about yourself and about us." He looked really sad as he said this.

"What is it?" I asked, sounding a little scared.

"First, look at your legs, dear," instructed my mother.

I didn't know what was going on, but I decided to follow her command. I removed the blanket that I was covered in and exposed my legs. When I saw my legs, I screamed. Earlier today they looked like an average set of legs on a person, but now my legs were completely abnormal! My legs were golden and had scales on them!

"What on Helmamnor happened to my legs?" I yelled.

"Dracollus," my father said, trying to sound reassuring, "Calm down and keep it down. Our neighbors will hear you."

"What's happening to me?"

"You're going through the changes of your transformation," my mother tried to explain.

"What transformation?" I asked, "I've already gone through puberty."

"Not that kind of transformation," my father said, "you're transforming into a…" he paused.

"Transforming into what?" I repeated.

"Into a dragon." He finished with a sigh.

"A dragon?" I asked, "Is this some kind of a joke?"

"That dragon you saw on the monitor, just now, Dracollus," my mother said, "that was you!"

"No, no that can't be right!"

"You've been a dragon since the day you were born," my father continued to explain. "You started to change into a dragon today."

"You mean," I said angrily, "you've known what I was going to be when I was born?"

"Well…" my father started off, only to let my mother continue.

"We have known about this, since the day you were given to us."

"Given to you?" I repeated confusedly, "What do you mean by that?"

"You are not our birth son," Lunfa explained, "You were given to me when you were still a baby by your father." I was so mad and anxious about this, but he continued, "Your father told me that we should protect you. He said that you had a very important destiny ahead of you."

I looked at them angrily. "You're…not…my…birth…parents?" I spoke, very annoyed. "You also knew I was something else, and you didn't tell me?"

"We were planning to tell you earlier today," Ilsa said. "We thought it was the best day to tell you these things."

"I had every right to know who I am!" I yelled. "Who my real family is and-"

At this moment Ilsa raised her hand. The second she did this my head started to hurt. It felt as if my brain was exploding from my skull. I put my hands to my head, and then groaned and moaned for a second. My mother put her hand down after a few minutes and at that instant, my head started to feel better.

"We were assigned to protect you for a reason," she said. "We know the ways of using magic."

"We stopped using it for almost a year until you came along," Lunfa said. "We've also had to make many sacrifices. We thought we should no longer use magic and try to live a 'normal' life here. We were sort of retired, then your father came to me and said that you were destined to change the world and that you would make the world a better place."

"Who was my father?" I asked. "And why did he leave me with you?"

Lunfa and Ilsa looked at each other nervously. "We'll tell you that when the time is right," Ilsa replied.

"No! You tell me now!" I demanded, "You've kept secrets from me for a long time, and I deserve the truth. Which reminds me, why did you decide to tell me the truth today?"

They were silent for a while, then Lunfa said, "We thought this day was the safest to tell you the truth because normally dragons don't change until seventeen cycles after their seventeenth birthday."

"Why is that?" I asked, still sounding a little demanding.

"I think we'll tell you more tomorrow, Dracollus," Ilsa said.

"No, I need answers now."

"And we need our rest. We are exhausted from trying to calm you down, and convert you back to a Helmam." Lunfa said.

Now that they mentioned it, they did sound tired, and they were in bad shape. "Ok, fine," I said, "But I need to know everything tomorrow."

Lunfa said, "We'll tell you as much as we know tomorrow. Now, have a good night, son."

"Don't you dare call me that!" I said angrily, "you may have raised me, but you are not my father."

"I am still your father," he explained patiently, "I may not be your birth father, but I was the one who made you who you are right now." They left the room.

When they were gone I started to realize that I could hear the electricity flowing through the light bulb. The electricity was buzzing and moving very loudly to me. It was very annoying, so I got out of my bed, turned the lights off and then went back to bed. I was starting to feel a little strange. After about a few minutes feeling nausea, it grew into a headache. I didn't know what to do, but I decided to get up from my bed and went to the kitchen to grab some water. As I was about to drink some water, the water felt like it was burning my mouth. I gagged and coughed instantly, and dropped my glass of water on the floor, which broke the second it reached the ground. My not-so-real parents came downstairs to see the problem.

"Dracollus," Ilsa asked, "what are you doing?"

I tried to explain, "I was feeling a little strange, then I got a headache, so I decided to come down here to get a drink of water, but when I tried to drink some-"

"Dracollus," Lunfa said, "your body has new cravings now that you are a dragon. Drinking water is no longer an opinion for you. If you need a drink, then drink this." He went to the refrigerator and handed me a bottle of beer.

"Lunfa," I said alarmed, "I'm too young to drink this stuff." The legal drinking age on our planet is 22.

"I know you are, but it's one of the things that can help you, so just drink it and be done with it."

I decided not to argue with him, so I took the bottle from him. I opened the bottle and took a swig. It tasted a little sour, but I liked it. I revolted at first, but I kept drinking. Before I knew it, I had finished the entire bottle. My headache was gone, but I was still feeling a little nauseous.

"Wow," I said sounding a little excited and drunk, "that was great."

"That's good," Ilsa said, "Now why don't you get some sleep so we can have our sleep." With that, they headed upstairs.

I went up to my bedroom, but I didn't go to bed. Instead, I went to my desk and got out my laptop. I went to see what was on the news about all the destruction I had caused. There were a lot of articles about buildings that were destroyed by burning in fire and the dragon in the sky. One article was about the history of the area and how there were no problems to ever happen there. In another one, there was an article about a temple that was destroyed, and they had a picture of what it was before the fire and after the destruction. It was the one I was at earlier. That's when I started to remember some of the events that happened today.

I recalled what happened at 17:17. The second I told Lunfa about fulfilling my destiny, I transformed into a dragon. I breathed fire toward the temple, and I rose to the sky using my new wings. I soared through the sky, breathing fire, and roaring every now and then. I could hear screaming from below and I saw people running in panic whenever I looked down. Some things were hurled up at me, like a fireball and a bolt of lightning. I guess that was Ilsa and Lunfa trying to get me tamed. The weather soon changed into a dark sky. I'm not sure if it was because of all the smoke coming from the burning buildings or if my "parents" were using magic to change the weather. I was just soaring through the air about to leave the area when this other dragon appeared in front of me. Well… it didn't just appear all of a sudden. It came flying through a great column of smoke. I don't know how it spoke to me but as soon as we dragons saw each other, a voice was in my mind saying in another language, "*Dracollus, calm down. You're causing a lot of havoc in this peaceful place.*"

Instead of heeding this message I just shot a column of fire at it. The other dragon dodged my attack. It then shot fire at my wing, and my wings were instantly damaged. I fell down to the ground very fast. I crash landed on a building that was made of bricks. The crash wasn't as painful as I thought it would be. The other dragon came towards me. Getting a better look at it, it appeared to be wearing some sort of crown on its head. The crown was made out of emerald, and it had rubies embedded in it. The dragon then started to shrink. It shrank until it became the size of a person, and after its size change, it morphed into a Helmam. The most shocking part was that I knew who this Helmam was. This Helmam-changed-dragon was Sylfano.

■■■

I groggily opened my eyes with a stiff neck, not realizing that I had fallen asleep sitting upright in my chair. I checked the time and it was 7:65 in the morning. The sun was starting to rise, which meant that I would get more answers about this *changing process*. Running downstairs to the kitchen, I grabbed cereal and milk, which I quickly devoured. I washed the bowl I used using rubber gloves. I was afraid of getting my skin wet all of a sudden. Maybe it was because I drank water last night, or maybe it was because I am now a dragon. I don't really know. I was feeling a little strange again, but I decided that I needed answers first before I do anything foolish. I proceeded to the room where Lunfa and Ilsa slept in and waited for them to come around. I waited for about an hour before Lunfa woke up. When he saw that I was in the room, he got out of bed.

"Go downstairs and wait for me there," he said quietly, "Let's give your mother a little more time to rest."

I went downstairs and waited for him at the kitchen table. When he got here, he was wearing a robe with special designs on it. "I need more answers now," I said.

"Alright," Lunfa said, "Now what is it that you want to know?"

"The first thing that I want to know is why didn't you guys tell me about what I am before these events happened?"

"Your mother and I told you last night."

"No, you and Ilsa said 'you thought it was the safest time to tell me on my birthday.' You never said why you thought it was the safest time to tell me."

Lunfa went to the refrigerator, opened the freezer and got out a box of frozen waffles. "We wanted you to have a happy life as a regular person, and not worry that you were going to be something different. If we told you what you are before, you might not have any friends and just have been hanging out by yourself. We also didn't tell you because it would attract some unwanted, and unwelcome attention to this peaceful land."

"And what kind of attention would that be?" I asked.

"You already know the answer to that," he said as he opened the box and put some waffles in the microwave.

I went through everything I knew about dragons in my head. I didn't know much about them. I knew that they could breathe fire, they're strong, have wings and have not been seen here in Housay for a very long time. I was trying to remember what it was that the dragons were so afraid of. Maybe sorcerers like my foster parents, but that didn't seem right because my birth father had given me to Ilsa and Lunfa when I was a baby. Then I remembered some stories Ilsa and Lunfa had told me when I was a young kid. The stories about how powerful the dragons are and how they want to live in a world of peace. They couldn't do that because of their enemies…

"The Gargoyles," I said out loud.

"That's right son." He said as he got the waffles out of the microwave, "If the gargoyles found out that there was a dragon living here in Housay, the war would be brought here, and after what my family and Ilsa's family has done for this place, it would disrespect them in so many ways. We took a huge risk by letting you live with us."

"What was the reason why you took me in as your child?" I asked.

"When your father came to me and asked me to raise you, I first refused, but then he told me that you had a very important role in a prophecy that was made many years ago."

"Who is my father?"

"He never told me his name nor did I do anything to find out more about him, but your mother had done some research on him for the past 17 years. She could tell you more about him when she wakes up.

Which reminds me, you need to go and tell your friends about the new you."

"Am I supposed to leave them now?" I asked nervously.

"That is for them to decide. They can be with you during your training, or they could leave you."

"What training?"

"You must learn to control your dragon form, and how to use to powers that have now awakened within you."

"Are you going to train me Lunfa?"

He smiled and said "No, son. I am not the one who is going to train you."

"So, Ilsa is going to train me."

"Oh no, neither of us are going to train you. Someone who is stricter and a lot meaner is going to train you."

I felt a little edgy at this news. "Who is it?"

Chapter 4

Secrets

I pulled out my portacall and first called Jamano. Mainly because I wanted to know if she was ok from the freaky fire incident. She picked up after the third ring.

"Dracollus," she said sounding really scared, "Are you alright? I never heard from you yesterday, and there was the attack."

"Calm down Jamano," I said as soothingly as I could, "I'm…OK, I guess."

"What do you mean by 'I guess'? Did something happen to you while the Ancient District was under attack by that dragon?"

"Look, just call Haruasore and tell him to meet us at the park in the Circle in 53 minutes."

"Ok, Dracollus, what is really going on? Because we never go to the Circle unless something really bad happens."

"I'll tell you guys when we are all together." I then hung up the portacall.

I didn't know what I was going to tell them. I left the house and walked to the Circle. The Circle is the most glorious place in the Middle District. The entire place is in a building about 71 krompus high and is shaped like a tall cylinder. I never found out exactly WHY this building is called The Circle in all my years living here. My best guess as to how this building got its name is because of the inside outlined is in a circle. The outside is mostly glass and windows but inside there are movies, arcades, stores and restaurants. There are about five floors in the building. Most of the restaurants are on the third floor, but there are a few restaurants on the second and fourth floor. The movies are, for obvious reasons, on the ground floor. On the top floor, the fifth floor is where all the security and head bosses' offices. If you want to work here at the Circle, then you will need to go to this floor and try to apply on this floor. As for the second, it is where the arcades section is. This means that the fourth floor is where the stores are located. The only times I hang out with my friends there is when one of our spirits is down. The last time I was here is when Jamano and Haruasore told me that they were a couple. They brought me here because they thought that I would be upset that they were an item, but they were wrong. I was totally relaxed when they spilled the beans. We all had a great time there. We watched a very funny movie, followed by lunch at a restaurant called Dark Kingdom, which is a hotdog restaurant.

Walking to the Circle usually takes me about an hour and a half, but according to my father, I could be at the Circle in 51 minutes if I jog. He said that now that I am a dragon, my speed would increase as well as my strength. I would learn more about my powers from my trainer, he reassured me. I wasn't certain if I was looking forward to meeting my trainer.

I jogged, and sure enough, I arrived in 51 minutes. If there wasn't a chance that my friends were going to leave me, I would have thought that this was awesome. I went to the park entrance of the Circle. The park is where trees grow under special lights around the center of the Circle. The park has walk paths, benches, some fountains, and statues of former guardians of Housay inside it. There are twenty-seven statues in the park altogether. My favorite statue in the park is the statue of Mutige. The reason why this statue is my favorite has to do a lot from what Ilsa has told me. Mutige was her great-grandfather. She narrated tales about him, and the most famous tale was his last battle, serving the guardians. In this tale, she described how he protected the high wall borders of Housay, with nothing but a sword made of steel. He killed about twenty stone-lords, dark sorcerers or sorcerous that serve gargoyles, and three gargoyles all by himself. He survived but was badly hurt, and he died a few months after that battle. The statue was erected in the Circle Park in his memory. The park itself is kind of small for such a big building. The entrance is at the base floor of the Circle. Everything else is either at or above the floor level of the park.

I kept pacing back and forth trying to decide what to tell my friends. I was solely focused on my thinking and before I could decide, I heard a voice saying, "Dracollus!"

I turned to see Jamano and Haruasore as they came running towards me. Jamano looked so worried, while Haruasore was calmly running towards me. When Jamano was really close to me, she held out her arms and then hugged me. When she did, I felt anxiety, worry, and fear radiating from her.

"I was so worried about what might have happened to you at the Ancient District," she said. "There was so much destruction that happened at that place."

"Thanks, Jamano and Haruasore. I'm totally fine," I said reassuringly. "But things are now a little complicated."

"Speaking of complicated," Haruasore said, "how was your date with Sylfano? We never heard from you."

"Can we please not talk about Sylfano at the moment?"

"*Oh my gosh*, the date went bad, didn't it? It was-"

"Guys, the date went well."

"But something happened, right?" He gasped as if he had a thought. "You guys kissed, didn't you?! You also mated with her!"

"Haruasore, seriously knock it off!" I was really mad that he was being his goofy self. I could feel his happiness as well. His silliness overcoming my own feelings.

Jamano gasped. "Dracollus," she said sounding very scared, "what's happening to your eyes?"

I took out my portacall and saw my reflection. In my reflection, I saw that my irises were glowing gold. After a few minutes, during which time I was able to relax, my eyes turned back to their original dark brown color. Looking at my reflection now, I realized that my black hair was a mess. It's usually neat and straight. Even with my eyes fixed on the reflection, I could feel Jamano's concern and fear. I turned my attention back to my friends.

"Hey, dude," said Haruasore sounding very concerned, "what happened to you?"

"That's what I've been trying to tell you guys, but you keep goofing off."

"So, what happened?" Jamano asked.

I took a breath before I explained, "You guys know about what happened in the Ancient District today?"

"Dude, don't tell me you were there when the dragon attacked?" Haruasore asked, sounding worried now.

"I was more than just be in that place when it was attacked."

"What do you mean?"

"I-" I paused to collect my thoughts. "I was the dragon that attacked the Ancient District."

"Wait, you were *WHAT*?!" Jamano exclaimed.

"I was the dragon," I repeated to her. "And if my eyes are not enough proof of what I am, this is." I then lifted up my sweat pants and showed them my golden legs. Jamano gasped shockingly. I sensed her total bewilderment emanating from her.

"Dracollus, how can you be a dragon? We've been friends for a long time and..." she paused horrified. She then looked like she was going to pass out at any minute. "Now it all makes sense. That's what your future was all about."

"What do you mean?" I quizzed her.

I expected her to respond, but I got a response from Haruasore. "Dude, you're a dragon?" He said sounding excited.

"Yeah, man, and it's not cool at all."

"Oh man, Dracollus," he now looked like he was going to blast off, "this is totally cool man. Since you're a dragon, it means that it was no coincidence that we meet. Or that we're friends."

"Dude cut it out man, this is not the time to act all goofy." I was starting to become very annoyed with him. Especially when his silliness was rubbing against my bad mood.

"***Hey man, I am not goofing off,***" he said in a really strange voice. "***I'm just trying to explain to you how this is only the beginning of our great journey together.***"

"***We don't have any journeys ahead of us Haruasore,***" I replied with the same strange voice, "***I am*** *going to be doing a lot of things now by myself. You and Jamano can only watch and encourage me while I do things, but you guys can't help me.*"

"Guys," Jamano asked sounding very clueless, "Why are you talking that way?"

It was only now that I realized I wasn't speaking Jarcannoph, our native tongue, but another language that I didn't know how I knew.

"*Why can't you*..." I stumbled trying to convert back to Jarcannoph.

"What was that?" asked Jamano.

"That was the ancient language of the Dragon," said a familiar voice that came from behind us. I turned around to see that incredibly, Sylfano was standing a few krompus away, with her arms folded to her chest. She had a couple of bruises on her arms but otherwise, she looked like her beautiful self, just looking bothered. I could literally feel how annoyed she was.

"Sylfano! I didn't know you were here. When did you get here?" I wondered exactly how she came from behind me since there was one entrance to the park and I was facing it.

"I was here way before you guys got here." As she said this I started to hear all the noises that were surrounding us. It was giving me a headache.

"Hey, Dracollus," Jamano said, "Are you alright?"

"Yeah, I'm fine," I reassured her.

"Dracollus, you are NOT alright." Sylfano said, "I know why you specifically chose this spot. You didn't want to hear surrounding sounds. Your hearing has been advanced now, so you can hear a lot of things no ordinary Helmam can hear. Like that popcorn machine on the left side of the Circle."

Now that she mentioned it, the popcorn machine was kind of annoying, but there were other sounds that I could hear which is kind of impossible for me to hear if I was a regular guy like Sylfano said. After a few minutes, I was able to block out all the surrounding noises again. When I came to my senses, I could hear Jamano saying,

"-a private conversation, Sylfano. You had no right to listen in."

"Actually," Sylfano said, "I have EVERY right to listen in on your conversation, considering all that happened yesterday."

"How much of our conversation did you hear Sylfano?" Haruasore asked her.

"I heard pretty much everything, and of course I believe all of you."

"You seem to know a lot about this whole dragon business Sylfano," Jamano said.

"Well, she should," I told her, "she is, after all, a dragon like me."

"*What?*" Jamano asked shocked.

"Ah," Sylfano sighed reassuringly, "so you do remember what happened yesterday."

"Not much actually Sylfano," I replied to her. "All I remember mostly about what happened that day was me turning in to a dragon, causing a lot of damage, and you turning from a dragon to… well, you."

"Yeah, that's the whole point of being a dragon." She told me. "You could either be a full-sized dragon, or you could be a Helmams. Which reminds me," she said as she faced Haruasore with a very skeptical look, "How could you speak the ancient language of the dragon? You're definitely not a dragon of any kind."

"No, I am not, your Highness." He spoke with a smile as if he had something he wanted to say that for a very long time. "I am not a dragon, but I am a dragon-lord."

"You're a what?" Jamano and I asked in unison.

"He's a dragon-lord." Sylfano repeated for him, "And if you're a dragon-lord that means you've known about who I am for a long time."

"Of course, your Highness. When word of your arrival got out on the streets, every dragon-lord was excited, but of course, we all had to keep your secret."

"Wait a minute, you two," Jamano interrupted. "What is it that the two of you are talking about?"

"Can we first start with what is a dragon-lord?" I implied.

Sylfano and Haruasore were quiet for a while. "Alright," he said at last.

"A dragon-lord is a Helmam that has dragon genes and some dragon powers. They know all about the ways of the dragon." Haruasore explained, "We can even speak the language of the dragon."

"What is so special about speaking the ancient language of the dragon?" Jamano asked curiously.

"If you can speak in the ancient language of the dragon that means all dragons will accept you as their kin, or their friend. Some of us dragon-lords are even trainers for other dragons."

"That is actually what my uncle, Jacob Mas Pal, is." Sylfano said, "Well, technically he is not my uncle."

"Yeah, he's your guardian," I interrupted her, "and your real father is actually the King of the Ancient Dragons, which means that you are the Princess of the Ancient Dragons."

Everybody was surprised at this, especially Sylfano. She looked as if I had just punched her in the gut.

"How did you know about my status as the princess?" she asked.

"More importantly," Haruasore said sounding extremely serious now, "how long have you known that Sylfano was the Princess of the Ancient Dragon Clan?"

I was a little nervous now that Haruasore was all being serious now. I was sweating a little bit.

"*I guess*..." I cleared my throat, and spoke in Jarcannoph, "I've only known, sorry I mean I *suspected*

Sylfano being a princess since yesterday when I remembered that your dragon was wearing a crown and when I saw a palace in your mind on our date. Also, the dream I had of you and your father kind of makes sense now."

"What dream are you talking about?" she asked skeptically.

I started to explain, "The night after our date I went to bed immediately. That night I-" I cut off when I thought someone was watching me. I turned around and looked up. It was at that moment that I saw Pireluve looking down from the third floor at me with a sinister look. He was leaning against the railing of that floor not looking good at all. I suspected that he was up to something.

"What are you looking at?" Jamano said.

I looked back at my friends and said, "I was just looking at… Hey, he's gone!" Where Pireluve was standing just a second ago, there was nobody.

"Who's gone?" Sylfano asked.

I looked at her for a second and then shook my head.

"Never mind." I said, "Moving on uh, where were we again?"

"You were explaining to us the dream you had," Jamano answered.

"Oh, right. I had this dream, well actually, I had two dreams."

I then told them about my dreams. Sylfano was wide-eyed the entire time I was talking. "You've dreamt all of this after our date?" she asked after I finished talking.

"Yeah, so what is all this stuff about you being here with a dragon-lord?" I asked. I was a little confused as to why she was here and what this would mean about us.

She was quiet for a while, and then she said, "I told you at the cafeteria that I came here because of the bad things my parents have done. That was no lie, as far as where we stand, Dracollus." She reached out and put her hand on my shoulder. I felt guilt, and regret coming from her.

"I never actually liked you, Dracollus," she said looking sad, "I did, however, enjoy our date."

"Wait," Jamano asked, concerned. "If you didn't actually like Dracollus, then why did you go out on a date with him?"

"That is a very good question Jamano. And the answer to that question is simple. I had a hunch that Dracollus was a dragon, so to see if my hunch was correct I went out with him on a date."

"What made you think that I was a dragon?" I asked, "I didn't find out that I was a dragon until my adoptive parents told me."

"And did they tell you what gave you away as a dragon?"

"No," I said. "I'm surprised that I can easily be identified as a dragon. What gave me away?"

Sylfano smiled amusedly, "It's your name. Draco is a common name for dragons."

"Is it really?" I asked, sounding really confused.

"Yes, it is," said Haruasore with confidence, "I question though why your parents named you as such - gargoyles can easily identify you as a dragon."

I was upset that Haruasore raised such a question, "Ok, first of all," I said angrily, "Lunfa and Ilsa are not my parents. Second of all, according to them, it was my birth father who named me Dracollus."

"Your birth father?" Jamano asked. She was clearly bewildered with this news. "What are you guys talking about now?"

I looked at Jamano and sighed heavily. "The day that I attacked the Ancient District, I blacked out most of the day. When I came around I found myself in my bedroom, and my adoptive parents told me about what I was and that they were given me by my birth father to protect me. According to them, my birth father claims that I have an important role to play in the future."

"Well yeah, that future may have to be put on hold," Sylfano said, "You guys should come to my house, so you can help cheer Dracollus when he starts his training."

"Who says he will train at your house?" Jamano asked her, looking a little upset. "Why can't he train at Haruasore's house where he knows the surroundings better?"

I answered for Sylfano. "That's because Haruasore is not the one training me."

"What do you mean Haruasore is not the one training you? He's your best friend and he's a dragon-lord. He's the most perfect choice to be your trainer."

Sylfano then held up her right hand and had all of her fingers pointing up, except for her fourth finger which was pointed down.

"Calm down, Jamano. Everything will be explained to you when we all get to my house."

"Well, can you start by explaining the meaning of that sign that you made with your hand?" Jamano asked her, but it sounded more like a demand than a question.

Sylfano looked a little shocked when she saw her hand. "Oh, I didn't mean to do this, but since I have already done it, the rest of you guys should know what it means." She then looked at me and continued to hold out her hand. "This means that I am a friend and I am unarmed and do not wish to cause harm. You should remember it because if you want to make treaties with the enemy, you need to know this symbol."

"Oh, OK," I said dumbly and I tried to copy her as best as I could.

"No, you're doing it wrong." She said sounding a little scared, "If you use your left hand that means you're armed, and if you're armed that means you mean to cause harm."

"Huh. That's an interesting way of remembering what the signs mean." I said with great confidence. I fixed my mistake.

"That is now correct. You're off to a good start. Now let us go to my house."

"Just so I'm clear," Jamano said as she pointed at Sylfano and Haruasore, "The two of you have been keeping this secret that Sylfano was a princess from me and Dracollus?"

Sylfano smiled and replied, "Well, to be honest with you guys, you always asked me questions about what happened to my parents, and never asked me about what my status was with my family. Or why I am not living with my parents anymore. Dracollus is the only one to have asked me these during our date. Although I did bend the truth a little bit because at the time I was not sure if Dracollus was a dragon."

"Speaking of the date," I said, "why did you really ask me on a date the other night?"

"I already told you-"

"That was not the entire truth about the date. You told us why you asked me on the date, but you never told us why you chose *that* specific restaurant. There is something that you are not telling us, and that is a secret I'd like to know now."

Sylfano looked a little disappointed. After a few minutes, she said, "I chose that location because I thought you were going to change at any minute. When I held your hand at lunch I immediately knew you were a dragon because you were experiencing my emotions. However, you have been showing signs that you are a dragon throughout this whole school year. You were a little faster and stronger then you were last year. I thought that the safest place for us to bond would be the *Red Dragon's Lair*, the restaurant that I live closest to here in the middle district. "Now," she said with a smile, "let's continue this conversation at my house."

Chapter 5

Learning about Dragons

"I have to say your house is awesome!" Haruasore said. "This place is the kind of place I could only imagine in my dreams. It's like a museum!"

Sylfano's house was huge! It was about the size of a school gymnasium. I expected that a house of this size would have a lot of rooms, but there were only eight rooms. There was Sylfano's, which was located on the second floor. Her room looked more like a hotel room because there were two queen size beds in there. Her room was the size of a classroom, with a walk-in closet across the entrance door. Her walk-in closet was half the size of her room, but it was still impressive. On the right half of the closet was where all the fancy clothes were while the other side was where the casual clothes were located. Inside her room was a desk about 7 krompus long. I wondered why she needed a desk that big. The rest of her room held bookshelves with all different kinds of books. Some were textbooks that a class would need, others were extremely old books (maybe even diaries by the look of the books), and about a handful of books that had no titles on them. In a connecting door, next to Sylfano's bedroom, was the master bathroom. In this bathroom, there was a sink that could be for two people and a toilet bowl. The biggest shock of the master bathroom was the hot tub in there as well as a shower stall. The hot tub looked like it could fit ten people in it. Even more shocking is how much space there still is for four people to move through the bathroom with all the space that is being taken up by the sink, shower stall, and the hot tub.

The next room across from hers is Jacob's. His room is small for such a big house. His room was the size of an average bedroom. He had a closet with a twin-size bed and a cabinet dresser. He had a small bookshelf in his room. The creepiest part of his room was that it was all purple. The wall paint was purple, the floor panels, his bed, and even his bookshelf with the books on it had purple cover pages. The next door was a bathroom. Not as grand as the master bathroom, but still a little bit as impressive. In this bathroom, there was a sink with a no-touch hands sensor. The toilet had an electronic on it as well. The shower also had electrical settings. I was quite impressed. Downstairs, on the ground floor, is the kitchen. There are three stoves counters, three ovens, and three refrigerators. I didn't even understand how a house would need to have three refrigerators for only two people. Then again, I surmised that since Sylfano is a dragon, perhaps her appetite is larger than an average Helmam. In the kitchen, there was an oddly shaped island counter in the center of the room. At the very back of the kitchen was a table that could seat about eight people. The floor panel was made of dark brown wood. Down the hall, close to the front door, there was a guest bedroom. This room was basically like Jacob's room, except that the room was green, the bed was red, and the floor was gray. There was a bathroom with only a sink and toilet right across where the guest room was located.

Her living room was about the size of a big gymnasium. It was basically half of the house. There was no floor above this place, which made more room for what was in it. The living room was filled with statues and pieces of artwork all over the place. Most of the artwork were paintings, which were hanging on the walls. There were so many paintings on the wall that showed only little bits of the blue walls, but there were some statues and sculptors in the room.

"I'm glad you like this place, Haruasore," Sylfano said, "Because not a lot of people like all this stuff that I have with me."

"People have come to your house before?" Jamano asked while she was still looking at a Waldarian painting with great awe at its beautiful details.

"Only the people that come to me to ask me on a date. There was this one time a girl came here and bumped into that statue that you are currently staring, at Dracollus."

"This is a really an interesting statue you have in your living room," I said, "It looks familiar."

"Yeah well, there are a lot of things here that look familiar to some people. Does anybody want something to drink?" she offered.

"Haruasore and I will have some water," Jamano said as Sylfano left to get drinks, "Are you allowed to drink water, Dracollus? I mean you do breathe fire out of your mouth and water is supposed to put out the fire in your mouth. Or is it your stomach?"

"I actually don't know the answer to that question." I said, "I am still new to this as well."

Sylfano came back with 2 bottles in each hand. In one hand, there were 2 bottles of water, in the other hand, she held 2 open bottles of beer. She gave the two water bottles to Haruasore and Jamano and gave me a bottle of beer. "Here you go, guys." she said enthusiastically, "Drink up Dracollus, you'll need it."

I opened the bottle of beer, took a swig, and felt better again.

"Dracollus," Jamano said, "You're still underage to be drinking that stuff!"

"He maybe underage as a Helmam, but he isn't as a dragon. A dragon becomes an adult and fully mature when it reaches the age of 17. So, bottoms up guys!" She then proceeded to drink some beer from the bottle she had in her hand. I drank more beer, and before I knew it, I had finished the whole bottle. "Drinking alcohol is the best thing for dragons because it makes our firepower stronger since alcohol is very flammable. There isn't much alcohol in beer, but for now, it will suffice."

I looked at the statue again, and I realized why it looked so familiar. It was a statue of her father, but the statue made him look a little bit older than when I saw him in my dreams.

"Why do you have a statue of your father in the living room?" I asked.

"That statue is to remind me what my father looks like. I have been away from him for four hundred years yesterday. I would hardly remember what he looks like if not for this statue."

"You've been away from him for HOW LONG?" Jamano exclaimed.

"Four hundred years. Jacob's great - to a number of degrees - grandfather, and I came to this land four hundred years ago."

"Wait," I interjected, "How old are you exactly?"

She smiled with great confidence and replied, "I'll be 1700 years old by the end of this month."

"But-"

"That is one of the powers of being a dragon Dracollus. Which is what Haruasore and I will tell you now."

"Can I explain the powers first?" Haruasore said with great courage and there was excitement in his eyes.

"Sure," she replied.

"Ok, so as Sylfano said before we got to her awesome and cool home, dragons are stronger and faster than a regular Helmam." He then reached for his pocket, "Like this fast."

He pulled his hand out and threw a knife towards my face. As if it was a reflex, I caught the blade with my right hand.

"HARUASORE!" Jamano shrieked as I put the knife on the living room table, "That could have killed him."

"It couldn't kill him," Sylfano said, "Dracollus can run quickly, and he has enhanced healing abilities."

As she said this, I noticed that my wound from the blade was no longer bleeding, though not yet healed completely. There was now a red line on my palm.

"These abilities are only the beginning of what we can do." Sylfano said, "We can do so much more. Our most gifted ability is the power of transpathy."

"Is that why I can feel everyone's emotion when I touch them?" I asked.

"Yes, it is. Later on, you will know how to turn it off, and how to use it without touching people."

"I think I get the hang of it now."

"Really?" Sylfano asked skeptically. "How could you?"

"This entire afternoon I have been feeling all your feelings whenever I want to, and I have never touched a single one of you today. Right now I am picking curiosity coming from both Jamano and you Sylfano. As for Haruasore, I can feel excitement from him."

"And you decide to tell us this just now?" Haruasore asked meanly.

"Well, the two of you," I pointed to Haruasore and Sylfano, "have been keeping secrets, so it's only fair that I inform you of this now."

Haruasore thought about it for a while, "I guess you're right," he admitted.

"Anyway, how can you still look like you are seventeen, even if you are really seventeen hundred years old?" I asked Sylfano.

"Same way as I can do this." She said as her face started to age a little bit more. Now she looked like she was in her mid-twenties. She looked so beautiful now. I guess becoming an adult can change things the way you look. After a few minutes, she became her regular self as a seventeen-year-old girl.

"Dragons can age shift." She properly explained. "We can be immortal in that kind of way. We can live for a long time and be any age we choose to be. Of course, we can die if we no longer choose to live, or we have our head cut off or something driven through our heart."

"Wow. That is a lot of stuff to remember," I commented.

"Fortunately for you Dracollus, dragons have amazing memories. We are able to remember a lot of things after only just briefly talking about it, or looking at it. We also have enhanced hearing, sight, smell and senses as abilities. As I mentioned before we are also transpathic. That is actually what I am doing now." Now that she mentions transpathy, I noticed that her lips were not moving, but I still heard her voice inside my head.

"Well, this is all interesting with the powers, but what a dragon's weakness, or weaknesses?"

"We'll get to that part," Haruasore said. "It's important to know your abilities rather than your weakness because you have more powers than weakness. The next set of powers is your skin. You have thick skin that can resist fire and most metals. You also have pyrokinesis, hence why and how Jamano had her hand on fire, but you didn't get burned. And yes at the time this happened, I was not aware that you were a dragon, so I did not know how to react. Anyway, moving on, dragons can also fly but only when they are in their dragon form."

"Which brings us to our next topic," Sylfano said in command again. "As you might already know, you have the ability to transform from a Helmam to a Dragon, and vice-versa. Your training on that subject will begin tomorrow."

"Why wait until tomorrow? Why can't Jacob train me today?"

"Wait," Jamano said, "Jacob is the one who will train Dracollus?"

"Of course," remarked the man himself, as he entered the room. "I have trained with Sylfano many times, and have gotten used to training dragons. Haruasore, on the other hand, has never trained a dragon, so he will have no experience with what to do."

"And truth be told," Haruasore said, "I am the worst dragon-lord of my generation."

"You are only saying that now, but when Dracollus starts his training you will become one of the greatest dragon-lords."

"That still doesn't answer my question about why I need to start training tomorrow," I persisted.

Sylfano looked sad, she almost looked like she was going to cry. "The answer to that question is part of the weakness of a dragon," she said. "Jacob, would you please explain to Dracollus?"

"Absolutely, your Highness. Dracollus, tonight is the night of the new moon. Dragons have powers thanks to the blue sun of our planet. At night, the only way for dragons to use their powers is from the light of the moon, so when there is no moon, dragons are powerless. That is why most gargoyle attacks take place during nights of the new moon. Since there is a new moon tonight we want you to have your powers ready, and be safe with your family."

"I would hardly call Ilsa and Lunfa my 'family'. They have been keeping things from me that I should have known for years."

"They were trying to protect you, just like how we kept our suspicions about you for years. Although we only tell you of our suspicions now, you are more hurt about your family keeping secrets about you because you feel betrayed by those whom you love. It is understandable to feel that way for now, but sooner or later, you must forgive them for trying to protect you.

"Now moving on - the next category of a dragon's weakness. The next weakness of a dragon is water. You may have already tried to drink water. Judging from the sour look on your face, you have tried this. Water disables the power of dragons to breath fire. The amount of water that you consume or get on yourself will determine how long you cannot breathe fire."

"You also have a weakness to high-pitched sounds. These sounds can or can't be heard by regular Helmams. As you experienced earlier, your hearing can be both a good and a bad thing. Any high-pitched sounds will hurt your ears. Some high-pitched sounds like the ones gargoyles use can make your ears bleed. You already know how to tune things out, so you don't need any training on that."

"The final weakness of a dragon is hellebore," he said as he pointed to the flower on the table where I put the knife that I caught. The flower was small and had white petals. "This…is a hellebore flower."

"What is so bad about this cute flower?" I inquired as I reached out for it.

The moment I touched it, I felt like I had just touched acid. I instantly pulled my fingers away from it. That's when I noticed that there was blood coming out of my hand. When I took a proper look at my hand,

I found that my wound from earlier had been cut open again, and now it was bleeding again.

"Hellebore weakens a dragon's ability to heal," he said as he wrapped my hand in a bandage cloth. "One touch and your healing abilities will be out for 34 minutes. It also makes dragons become a little weaker. That is the most important weakness to remember."

"Oh, Jacob," Sylfano said, "You forgot the material that kills dragons!"

"Oh, right! I always keep forgetting that. The last and final weakness of dragons is the substance that can kill a dragon: obsidian. It is the only known piece of matter that will kill you because if a dragon is cut by obsidian the wound will never heal. That is why you will never find any obsidian here. The princess should never have to fight against obsidian swords here. We have only one obsidian sword though, but that sword is well-hidden somewhere in the Industrial Area. I am the only one who knows where it is located. The reason I have it is to use it only as a last resort of violence against a dragon.

"Anyway, I am getting side-tracked. You should go back to your home and get some rest for your training tomorrow."

"Fine, but can I go home after I have something to eat? I'm starving."

I got home pretty late. The sun was almost setting when I arrived home. The jog I took from the Red Dragon's Lair and then to my house was more tiring than what I had expected. I made it home at 5:67, and I was breathing hard and sweating a little. I guess jogging 17 dlaus from the Red Dragon's Lair can make a regular Helmam be out of breath and sweating like crazy. But for a dragon, that means nothing. I guess that since this is a new moon day, I was feeling weaker because my powers were starting to diminish. The Hellebore flower weakness had been gone for 2 hours. I opened the door to my house and found out that I could not get in. It was like there was an invisible barrier in front of me.

"ILSA, LUNFA!" I yelled so they could hear me.

My mother came to the door first followed by my father. "Dracollus, we are so glad you're home!" She said, "We were getting worried that you might not make it before the sun had set. Come in, please."

"Speaking of setting," I said staying still, "did you guys set up any magical barriers here, because I can't come in."

My father looked a little confused, but more surprised.

"That's strange," he said, "The barrier is meant to keep out gargoyles from coming in the house only. A dragon such as yourself should pass the barrier with no problem."

I was confused, but when I tried to enter the house again, it worked.

"*That was a little odd,*" I said.

"What did you say?" my father asked.

At first, I was surprised that he couldn't understand me, but then I realized I had spoken in a different language. This was not the Ancient Language of the Dragon. It was another one, and I didn't know what that language was at the time.

I cleared my throat, "I said 'that was a little odd'."

"What language was that you said it in?" my mother asked. "It didn't sound like the ancient language of the dragon."

"I don't know," I said dumbly.

"Alright. Well, are you hungry?"

"Actually, I already ate," I said as I took a seat in the kitchen. "After I left Sylfano's house, I went to the Red Dragon's Lair and had dinner with Jamano, Haruasore, Sylfano, and Jacob Mas Pal."

"Wait, when did you go to Sylfano's house?" my father asked.

I took a deep breath and told them what happened today: how Haruasore is a dragon-lord (they were really surprised about it), how Sylfano is the princess of the ancient dragons (this did not surprise them), how I learned the powers of being a dragon, and what transpired the moment I touched the hellebore flower.

"Well, things are going better than I expected," my father said. "Not only do you have both your friends by your side, but you are also able to control some of your powers already."

"Yeah, things are better now that I know a lot in such a short period of time."

"Actually, my son," my mother said, "there is something else the princess forgot to tell you that's important, and I think it is the reason that you transformed early."

"What is it?" I asked, sounding and looking very curious.

"You changed on the 17th second of the 17th minute of the 17th hour of the 17th day of the 17th month of the 17th year of the 17th century. In other words; you changed on 1717 at 17:17:17."

"What is the deal with all those seventeens?"

"Dragons are all about power and order," my father explained. "For dragons, the number seventeen represents power. The more seventeens there are in a dragon's age, the more powerful the dragon is. We suspect that since there were so many seventeens on your birthday, those triggered your dragon powers to become so powerful that you were not able to control it, and your transformation."

"Is that what really happened? Or are you just guessing?"

"Like we said before," said my father. "We are only theorizing what caused your sudden transformation…"

They continued speaking, but to me, their words were starting to sound funny, and I realized that the room was starting to spin, then everything went dark.

As soon as I could see again, I knew it was a dream. I saw myself standing at what looked like an abandoned power plant, throwing fire at some tin cans with Sylfano, Jacob, Haruasore, and Jamano watching me. The way I was throwing fire it looked as if I had just begun training. After I shot down all the cans, Haruasore went over to pick them up and put them even farther. Then, just as Haruasore was about to come back, I started to sneeze. Everyone ran in different directions. I sneezed and what should have been just a sneeze turned into something more. When I sneezed, I shot out what looked like an icicle, and I pierced a tin can. The dream then shifted into something even more frightening. I was lying on the ground and Sylfano was on her knees. We looked like we were in the Forest District but the place looked as if an explosion went off, like the day I caused so much damage in the Ancient District. Sylfano was trying really hard to stand up, but she just could not. It was as if she didn't have enough strength to lift herself up. Then Pireluve came into the dream. He was holding a black sword, which was about a 3 krompus long, in his left hand, and a black shield with a gray gargoyle embedded in it, in his right hand. He charged at Sylfano from behind. When he was about 20 krompus away from her, I was able to stand up. I looked at him and saw that he was going to strike her heart. I said something, but I couldn't hear what it was. I then ran towards him as fast as I could. When he was 5 krompus away from her, I got behind Sylfano. Instead of striking Sylfano's heart, he struck my chest!

The scene changed to the same room that I had the night of my date. I was once again in the room full of fire, only this time the flames were not hot at all, they were actually quite cold. I went to the other side of the room to find a red dragon all curled up. For some reason, the dragon looked familiar, even though I had never seen it before my last dream. Something about the dragon's face haunted me. I felt like I should be able to place this dragon somewhere, but I just couldn't. The dragon was at sleeping first, but when I came close to it, it grabbed me. The dragon woke up and said to me, "**_That was only the beginning of your future, the rest is much more dangerous, and you will find a much darker secret._**" At that point, I woke up.

My father was at my bedside, and I was once again in bed. I sat up feeling kind of weak from last night.

"Good morning Dracollus," he said. "How are you, and how was your sleep?"

"I feel kind of weak," I said with a weak voice. "That new moon really got the best of me."

"That's the kind of thing that happens to dragons."

"Speaking of dragons, is it normal for a dragon to have strange dreams?"

My father smiled, "Dragons dream differently than Helmams do. Dragons dream of the present, what is happening to their friends and loved ones. Sylfano may or may not have told you that, because it is not a major power. It is more of a special gift that dragons possess."

"Ok, but do dragons dream of the future?"

"What do you mean the future?"

I described to him all of my dreams, except the part where I had a sword driven through my heart (that part still scared me so I didn't want to say it). I told him about the red dragon and how the dragon said that my dreams were all about my future. My father was quiet and looked pensive for a long time. Then he said,

"It seems like you have the ability to dream of the future. That is something you should have told Sylfano."

"I only learned of this from my dream last night. Why should have I told Sylfano this? Can't she see the future in her dreams?"

"No, she cannot," he said, sounding very serious. "I heard that there is only one other dragon that can see the future and not just in his dreams, but this dragon has the vision of seeing the future. This dragon is the Ancient Prophet of the Dragons."

"Who is that dragon? And where can I find him?" I was curious as to what that meant for me. Was I related to this dragon? Are we connected in some way? Could he find my father? Could he answer why I kept seeing a red dragon in my dreams?

My father said, "Go to Sylfano and tell her all of these things before your training begins. She must know about this. As for the prophet of the dragons," he paused to gain his thoughts. "No one and I mean NO ONE knows where the prophet dragon is."

"Why is that?"

My father remained silent for a while. "Just go to Sylfano's house, and tell her everything you told me. You can even tell your friends if you want them to know what is going on."

Chapter 6

Focus and Knowledge

"That is very interesting," Sylfano replied after I told her what I had told my father. I didn't tell her that I would have a sword driven through my chest as I didn't trust anybody, not even my two best friends, with that information.

"It seems like you have the potential to be the next dragon prophet. This would be a really good change. It would also explain how you are able to control some of your powers already."

"Do you know where I can find the Dragon Prophet?" I asked her

"I would not even have the slightest clue as to where he is now. I only met the Ancient Dragon Prophet a couple of times before I left the Kingdom of the Ancient Dragons. Last I saw him, he was just coming back from a diplomatic meeting with the Former Queen of the Ancient Gargoyles. According to my father about eighteen and a half years ago, he disappeared."

"Where did he go? Why did he just disappear?"

"No one knows except for the King of the Ancient Dragons," Jacob said, "and the only way for you to see the King is if you are the princess or have important news about the war. In either case, you cannot see the King right now."

I was vexed that I could not see the King or the Dragon prophet. "Do you know what the Dragon prophet looks like in his Helmam form at least?" I asked, sounding eager to have an answer.

"I wouldn't remember. It's been so long ago that I can't remember. The only thing that I remember is that when you look into his eyes you would feel despair. Despair that knowing something dark was around the corner close to you. But enough of this, you have some work to do. Let Jacob…"

"Shouldn't Dracollus warm up first?" Jamano asked Sylfano.

"That's what I am going to show him," said Jacob. "And technically, he does not need to warm up. All he will do is mediate."

"Is that all that I'll be doing today?" I asked skeptically.

"That is not the only thing you are going to be doing, of course, but your first lesson of training is going to be how to phase shift into a dragon and back to a Helmam."

"Trust me," Sylfano said, "At first it is extremely difficult to do. Once you get the hang of it, you'll be able to transform into something else."

"Into what?"

"When you have mastered the ability to shift into a dragon, then I will tell you."

"Now," Jacob said, "I want you to close your eyes and focus on my words."

I closed my eyes. He said, "Now focus on being a dragon. Think of nothing else but being a dragon. Let nothing distract you."

I did what he told me.

"Are you doing it?"

I nodded my head. At that moment, I felt like something had hit my head. I opened my eyes instantly.

"You should let nothing distract you," Jacob said "not even a hit to your head. You NEED to keep your focus on being a dragon, or you'll turn back into a Helmam. Only when you have absolute focus can you achieve the full transformation."

"Ok, I'll try again," I said.

"No, don't try. Do it." Haruasore said.

We all looked at Haruasore.

"What?" he asked us, confused.

"You are not the one training me," I said, "so don't command or give orders to me."

"I was not commanding. I was merely stating a comment," he explained.

I sat on the ground, crossed my legs, meditated and focused on trying to be a dragon. I imagined that I was transforming into a dragon, flying through the skies, breathing fire and-

"Dracollus, open your eyes," Jacob said. I knew better than to listen to him this time. I continued to focus on being a dragon.

"Dracollus that's enough meditating," Sylfano said.

I opened my eyes, but I continued to keep focused on being a dragon.

"You can stop believing that you're a dragon now," Jacob said. "Look at your hands and see the progress you have made."

I looked at my hand and was so shocked that I stopped believing that I was a dragon for a brief second. My nails on my fingers had turned into long, black claws. But then they turned back into nails.

"That was awesome," I said. "I transformed my fingers after only meditating for a few minutes."

"A few minutes," Jamano spoke skeptically. "Dracollus, you have been meditating for 42 minutes."

"I have?" I checked my portacall for the time and sure enough, 42 minutes had passed. "Well, that was…"

"Confusing and interesting," Sylfano said, finishing my sentence. "Yes, I know. The first time I did it was very confusing, but it was also interesting. You are progressing really fast. It took me cycles to complete the transformation of my nails, but it only took you minutes. However, the tricky part is yet to come - that would be transforming into your actual dragon form. It took me weeks and a lot of patience to do it. I even had to stay up a couple of nights."

"Does that mean I have to?"

"Yes, and no," Jacob replied. "If you can transform within the next two weeks you will not have to stay up any nights."

"Do you guys really expect me to do it within the given time limit?"

"Yes, we do. You have made so much progress that we think that you can do it."

"This is a lot of pressure on me now."

"There is no pressure, but if you feel like there is you can run around the house thirty times to let some fire out, so to speak."

"Alright, I'll do that. It will give me a chance to stretch my legs."

Running around the house was easy. The house was huge and very wide, but I was able to run around the place thirty times. I even tried believing that I was a dragon while I was running.

I would continue to run and meditate for a whole week.

"Come on, Dracollus," Jacob yelled. "Stop believing you are a dragon and change into a dragon already!"

"WILL YOU CUT IT OUT?" I exclaimed and stopped running, "I have been trying to transform for eight and a half cycles now. I am doing the best I can to transform. I am getting tired of your yelling."

"You will be running for your life if you can't transform into a dragon."

"Yeah, well when I do transform, I will most likely be something that can be..." I paused to regain my thoughts.

"That can be what?"

"That can be something to shut you up!"

After 30 laps around the house, I began to meditate. This time, I tried to will my body to change into a dragon. The previous times I just imagined and believed that I was a dragon. Now I am trying, no I AM willing my body to change. After what seemed like a few minutes, I felt my insides were exploding. This was completely different from what I felt the first time I transformed on my birthday. When I opened my eyes, the world looked somewhat smaller. I looked at my hands and discovered that golden scales have covered my hands. My dragon claws were out. My nose was turning into a dragon's snout. My legs were becoming bigger. I stood up only for a brief second, and then my transformation was complete. My body had expanded and became that of a dragon's. I had a tail, and wings grew from my shoulder blades. I put my transformed paws on the ground; it seemed like the natural thing do. I walked towards Sylfano, Jacob Mas Pal, Jamano and Haruasore.

"This is the new me," I said to all of them transpathically.

Everybody applauded for me, especially Haruasore, who was rooting for me.

"Excellent job, Dracollus!" Sylfano said with a mischievous look on her face.

"What's wrong?" I asked transpathically, "You're looking at me with a mean look."

"Oh, it's not you I'm looking at. It's your wings that I'm looking at with this look."

I spread my wings to check them. They were about three krompus long, and they looked like what I thought were dragon wings.

"What's wrong with them?"

"Your wings are bat wings." Jacob said, "Normally, wings of a dragon have scales on them, and sometimes they have feathers like a bird's, but no dragon has ever had bat wings. Your wings look almost like a gargoyle's."

"Speaking of gargoyles, it's time you learned the different types of gargoyles," Sylfano said. "There are three different types of gargoyles; the omegas, the deltas, and the gammas. The omegas are the leaders of a flock of gargoyles. Deltas are the basic foot soldiers of a flock. You can tell the difference between the omegas and the deltas from their wings. The omegas have their wings on their shoulder blades, while the deltas have their wings protruding from their arms. The last of the gargoyles are the gammas. Gammas are basically loners, they either choose to be alone or they are the last surviving members of a flock that was defeated. It is rare to meet a gamma since gargoyles are stronger in flocks. I almost forgot to tell gargoyles usually come in flocks of seven to seventeen. It's important that you know what you are dealing when it comes to a flock. Then you must know the different kinds of gargoyles. The first is the most important one of all; the Ancient Gargoyles. These gargoyles are the descendants of the first ever known gargoyles. If you ever meet an Ancient Gargoyle, don't try to fight it. You just run away and don't look back. Ancient gargoyles can't be killed at all. Nobody knows how to kill an Ancient. However, the average gargoyle, which are called Converters or Verts for short, can be killed. They can be killed like a Helmam, but if they are killed by sapphire, they will become a pile of ash. The last kind of gargoyles are the Summoned Gargoyles. These gargoyles can only exist on Helmamnor for a short amount a time. It depends on the Summoner to determine how long Summoned Gargoyles will stay on Helmamnor.

"But enough of that, I think it's time to tell your parents the good news."

Chapter 7

More Training

"Well done, Dracollus!" my mother exclaimed when I told her the good news. "You sure have worked hard in transforming into a dragon."

"You," my father said, "have trained only for a short amount of time, and you have already mastered your transformation. You are a very special dragon."

"A special dragon that is extremely tired." I said, "I'd like to go to sleep if you guys don't mind."

"Oh, of course," my mother replied. "All that training can make someone tired, and jogging back straight from Sylfano's house should be exhausting. You can go to your bedroom now."

"Pleasant dreams, I hope," my father said. I went upstairs to my room and changed into my pajamas before getting into bed.

In my dream, I saw myself transforming into a dragon and flying into the darkness, which I assumed was the night sky. I then followed a purple or blue dragon; it was difficult to tell. Anyway, I followed the other dragon into some clouds. It dodged certain clouds in the sky. I followed it as best as I could but got behind since encountered thick clouds. Eventually, the dragon landed in what I thought was the Forest District. When I landed, I had a better look at the dragon. I noticed an emerald crown with rubies embedded on it, and at that precise time, the dragon changed into Sylfano. I realized that Sylfano was guiding me and teaching me how to fly carefully.

Suddenly my dream changed. Jamano and Haruasore were in front of Sylfano's house. "That was wicked awesome to see wasn't it?" Haruasore told Jamano.

"Yeah, it was," she replied. "I have never seen a Helmam transform into a dragon. I bet you have, being a dragon-lord and all that."

"Truth be told, I have only seen one other dragon transform, and that was Sylfano, on the day of Dracollus' birthday."

"How come?" she inquired.

"There aren't any dragons here in Housay, except for her Highness and Dracollus."

"So you were there at the Ancient District when Dracollus transformed?"

"Did I say I saw her transform the day of Dracollus' birthday? No, I meant the day before Dracollus' birthday. I followed Dracollus after they left the *Red Dragon's Lair*. I followed them."

"Haruasore! You didn't!"

"I know how it sounds, but I wanted to know where the princess lived. Anyway, when Dracollus left, she changed into a dragon and I left immediately because I was afraid that after she changed so she could find me."

"How couldn't she find you if you were right there?"

"I was close to Sylfano's house but I was farther than regular hearing range."

"What do you mean regular hearing range?"

"Oh yeah, that's right - I forgot to tell you, Dragon-lords have much better hearing than dragons do. We can turn our advance hearing on and off whenever we want to."

"That sounds so cool." She then leaned to him and kissed him.

The scene changed into a room of an old-fashioned castle. I was in the throne room, hiding. There were 5 Helmams in the room. One of them was on the throne, so I assumed she was the queen, and two Helmams were by her side, acting as guards. The other two men were standing in front of her.

"How are the preparations for the invasion of Housay?" the queen asked.

"There has been a little setback, your Highness," one of the Helmams in front of her replied.

"What KIND of setback Mogirth?" the queen demanded.

"Well," said Mogirth, "According to our spy there is another Dragon there in Housay, but there is nothing to worry about, your Highness. This dragon just turned 17 some time ago, so the princess and her guardian will be distracted and focusing on training this new dragon. As you can see-"

"What is the name of this new dragon?" The queen asked, interrupting Mogirth.

The other men kneeled before the queen.

"I am sorry, your Highness," he admitted, "but we do not know the identity of this new dragon. Our spy has been looking for this new dragon's identity for the past 9 cycles and nights. Please forgive us."

The queen was upset at this news, but she looked more concerned. "When did this our spy find out that there was another dragon at Housay?"

Mogirth said to her, "He found out on the 17th of this month, your highness."

The queen was shocked by this news but Mogirth and the other man did not seem to notice.

"The dragon caused a lot of destruction to Housay. He made our jobs of destroying Housay a little easier. It could have been that the dragon was on our side, but according to the spy, this was the dragon's first time transforming. When our spy finds the out identity of this other dragon, he will kill him."

"That is all very good news to me. Now, my guards will escort you to the dining room where you two will discuss with the other members on what to do when the defenses are down."

"But your majesty-" Her guards tried to object.

"You will escort them to the dining room. I wish to be left alone for a few minutes."

"As you wish, your majesty." They all left the room.

When they were all out of the room the queen stood up from her throne and walked around the room.

She kept walking in circles as if she was thinking about something important and just could not place it. All of a sudden, she stopped and straightened herself. She looked at me, or at least I thought she was looking at me. I confirmed that she was looking at me when she said,

"*I hope they don't find out the truth about you Dracollus.*" She then changed into a gargoyle.

I opened my eyes to find that Sylfano was sitting by my bedside. The sun was still up when I woke up, so I thought that I only slept for a few minutes.

"How did you sleep?" she asked me with a smile.

"I slept well, thank you. What are you doing here?"

"I'll answer that in a minute, but first tell me your dream. What were they about?"

"Well," I told her my dreams, except for the last one. I didn't want her to worry that an invasion was on its way to Housay when she was so focused on getting me proper training.

"Well, it seems as if your dreams constantly shift from the future to the present, or your dreams change randomly."

"Maybe, but I still don't know how these dreams of the future are going to help us with my training. Speaking of which, are you here to help me train more?"

"Yes and no. I'm here to show you where it is we are going to train. Jacob and I thought of a better place for you to train now that you are a full-grown dragon."

"Where is this place that you are taking me?"

"I'll show you after you had some mornfast. I have to say your father makes one of the best Awe Eggs Sandwiches I have ever had."

"Yeah, he does make good… Wait. You just had mornfast here. What time is it?"

"The time is 7:62 in the morning, and yes, I just had mornfast."

DANG, I thought, I slept through the rest of the day and the whole night too. Transforming into a dragon really took a lot of energy out of me. This was worse than the night of the new moon.

"You don't always use a lot of energy," Sylfano said as she read my emotions. "The first and second times you transform are always the hardest and the most tiresome."

"So it gets easier to transform?"

"Yes, it does. Now let's get you some mornfast before doing our long fast run to the Industrial District."

I had a good mornfast of ham, sunny side up eggs and Housay bread. When I finished, Sylfano met me at the front door. She sure was ready to leave in a hurry. "Come on, Dracollus," she said to prove my point.

"Where are we going that you have to hurry me up?"

"We are going to the Industrial District, and we are running there."

"WE ARE RUNNING THERE?" I asked skeptically.

"Oh yeah. I knew I forgot to tell you something, Dracollus. Dragons are more endurable than Helmams."

"So in other words, we can run super-fast-"

"We can run very fast. I should be able to run faster than you because I'm a member of the Ancient Dragon Clan. The members of the Ancient Dragon Clan are faster than regular dragons, and the older the dragon is, the stronger and faster it becomes."

"Ok. So anyway," I continued, "We can run super-fast and can run to a place that is hundreds of dlaus away from here?"

"Yes," she said reassuringly. "That's right. NOW try and catch me, *IF you can*." She taunted me. And then she disappeared into a blur. I ran after her. The background became a blur, and I caught up to Sylfano quickly. I didn't hit any transports or buildings because I could sense when I was approaching them dlaus away. I can't really describe how I knew they were coming. All I can say is the feeling is like being in a crowded room. When someone says something to you, you just know it was meant for you. That is something like how I could tell there was a building in the way. Sylfano tried to run a little bit faster, but I was able to catch up with her. I could not believe my speed!

We arrived at the Industrial District before I knew it. For one spilt millisecond time seemed to have slowed. Everything was not moving, not even Sylfano. She seemed to have stopped moving altogether. When I looked around I saw a sign on my left that said, 'ENTERING THE INDUSTRIAL DISTRICT'. After I had finished reading the sign, I looked to my right and saw one of the most famous landmarks of the Industrial District the Monument that Lead Creation. This Monument was just a simple pillar made of a very rare metal here on my world. You would call it lead. Lead is extremely rare to find in my world. About one out of a thousand mines can find even little trace amounts of lead in them. The Monument is a symbol that when the Industrial District was founded, the very first things to be made were made of lead. Looking at this monument made me smile.

Time seemed to have resumed, and I was moving with blinding speed. I didn't know when to stop, so I looked at Sylfano for guidance. While we were running her hair kept swinging back and forth in a very nice way. The way she ran was more interesting than me transforming into a dragon. She was more beautiful running with super speed than when she is just standing still. When she looked at me finally she smiled, then told me transpathically, "It's time to stop." I slowed down to reduce my speed, and then I stopped.

I was breathing hard after my run, but I was able to look at the place where Sylfano and I had arrived. We were at an old abandoned power plant. The place looked like it had been hit by a storm. There were walls of buildings half destroyed. Doors were lying on the ground. There was glass all over the place, and there was no roof on any of the buildings. I wonder what kind of training we would do here. There were a whole bunch of transports in the parking lot, which all were in bad condition, and stone bumpers that were all lined up differently. There was only one building that was completely intact. The blue door to that building opened up, and out came Haruasore, Jamano, and Jacob. My friends ran towards me and hugged me.

"That was awesome!" Jamano said. "You ran over 221 dlaus in only 28 minutes. How cool is that?"

"How did you know that we were running here?" I asked with great enthusiasm.

"Your portacall has a tracking system." Haruasore said, "Jacob here showed us how to access them. It was really interesting seeing you run that fast."

"It was more interesting catching up to Sylfano here."

"Which SHOULD be impossible, actually," she said, sounding concerned.

"What do you mean, your Highness?" Jacob said to her.

She looked at me still looking concerned, "You ran as fast as me, if not faster. You were able to catch up to me and ran by my side. That is something not possible. The only dragons that should be faster than me are my parents. Even if you are an ancient dragon you still should not be faster than me, because I am way older than you."

"Oh great," I said "that makes five different things already. I wonder if I will have seven different things that are different from being a regular dragon."

"Five?" Haruasore asked while counting with his fingers, "I counted three different things about you. What are the five different things about you?"

"Well for starters, I transformed on my 17th birthday, which by the way is seventeen cycles earlier than when a normal dragon should have turned. I transformed for the seconded time in only a matter of cycles instead of weeks. I have bat wings instead of dragon wings and no dragon has had bat wings before me. I can dream of the future, which only one other dragon can do by the way. Finally, I am faster than an ancient dragon that is 1700 years old. If you add all those together, you get 5. I am getting tired of being so different!"

"Dracollus," Sylfano said as she put her hand on my shoulder, "calm down. Your eyes are glowing gold, which would indicate that you are going to turn soon."

I sat down, closed my eyes in concentration and mediated for a while before I was able to calm down. I then opened my eyes and stood up.

"Ok," I said casually. "What's next? I mean, what kind of training will I be doing here?"

"You'll be tested on your strength and your pyrokinesis aim here," Jacob said. "We will first start with your strength. Please follow me."

Jacob moved ahead of us and walked off in a hurry. We all followed him toward the other side of the plant. On the other side of the plant, there was a big wall that was at least 50 krompus tall. It blocked the view of what was on the other side of the wall. Against the wall were over a dozen transport wheels that had spray painted gold rims. Two of the wheels were still connected with an axle. There was a stack of wheels of six next to the wheels with the axel and the rest were scattered. There was a bench-pressing gym set with no bar or weights. I wonder how Jacob was going to train me with weights if there were only transport wheels to lift.

"So how exactly are you guys going to train me? I am supposed to lift each wheel and make another stack?"

"Yes and no," Sylfano said. "You only stack the wheels only as a warm-up. That axel," She pointed to the axel, "is what you are going to be lifting."

"I want you to lift a rim from the stack and make a new stack," Jacob said.

I walked over to the stack, and when I tried to pull the top wheel, I almost fell. The wheel was so heavy that I couldn't move it. I tried to pull and then push the top wheel for a few minutes until I finally gave up.

"Why are these wheels so heavy?" I asked, almost out of breath.

"The rims of the wheels are not spray painted gold," said Jacob. "They are actually made of solid gold. 100% twenty-four karat gold rims. One tire wheel should weigh about two and a quarter tons. This is how your strength will be tested."

"OK, now you are trying to push me."

I took off my shirt because I thought it would help me a little. I then tried to lift the top rim up again. I still could not. After a while with no success, I stopped for a second and put my hands on my knees.

"Come on, Dracollus," Haruasore yelled, encouraging me. "You can do this! Use your inner dragon strength to lift the rim!"

"Ok, Haruasore. I'll do it."

I gave it another go, only this time I concentrated on using a lot more strength. I imagined that I had more strength to lift the rim above my head. I KNEW I was stronger than a regular Helmam, and I knew I could lift this golden wheel. I did it once more and lifted the wheel above my head.

"I did it!" I exclaimed in a joyful and relieved tone.

"That's good," Jacob said. "Now, move the wheel to the other side of the wall and make a new stack." I followed his instructions, and I kept removing the rims from the old stack to a newer one. When I was done I looked at Sylfano and asked, "What next?"

"Next," she smiled, "we get you in better shape!"

Chapter 8

Fire and Sound

"Excellent job, Dracollus!" Sylfano said to me as I finished my last set of bench presses.

I have been training and lifting weights for six weeks already. I have been transformed from a thin, scrawny Helmam to a battle-ready warrior, or so I hoped.

"Thanks, Sylfano," I said. "All this hard work is getting easier to do now that I know how to summon my inner dragon strength."

"That's great to hear." Jacob Mas Pal said. "What about you, Haruasore? How are you doing?"

Haruasore had been training in weights on his own for three weeks. Not that he needed to get in shape since he was already in shape. He trained because he needed to increase his strength. I soon found out that dragon-lords are stronger than Helmams but are weaker than dragons. Jacob wanted to Haruasore stronger in case he encountered any wild or rogue dragons. When Haruasore started training, he could only lift 100 pounds on each side, but now he is able to lift 250 pounds.

"Things are going great for me," Haruasore replied as he continued his dumbbells. "I'm stronger now, and that makes me happy, but can you guys please be a bit quiet? I really want to finish my set and you are all distracting me."

We all remained silent as Haruasore finished his last set. Then he put his weights down and breathed heavily. When he was breathing normally again, Jamano hugged him.

"You did a great job today," she exclaimed to her boyfriend. "If you keep this up, you will be lifting 280-pound weights by the beginning of the next month!"

"Unfortunately, he won't have to lift additional weights." Jacob said, "It is now time for Dracollus to learn about his different fire throwing capabilities and how to control each of them."

"Different fire throwing capabilities?" I asked Jacob and Sylfano, "Why should I learn the different ways of hurling some fire from my hand? Oh, and when will I actually get some real training? When will you guys teach me how to fight? Pardon me for being a little impatient, but I have been patient since the beginning of training. I thought you guys were supposed to teach me how to defend myself!"

I sounded a bit irritated, but I had been working my butt off for the past seven weeks of training, and not once did they show me any fighting move for self-defense.

"We are going to teach you on how to defend yourself." Sylfano said, "But we don't have to teach you how to fight. You already know how to do that!"

"I do?" I asked, skeptically.

"Yes, you do."

"And how did I learn Kung Fu or other self-defensive moves, exactly?"

"Observe," Jacob said as he pulled a knife out of his pocket. The knife blade was blue and it glowed a little. It looked like a blade used for ceremonies. I didn't think it would hurt me, but then again my skin would break the blade if it touched my skin.

"Wait, Wait, Wait!!" I exclaimed holding my hands up, "If you're going to throw that blade at me, I already know how fast I am and we all know that I can catch the knife."

"I know that you can catch it. I was going to see how well you can defend yourself."

With that, he lunged at me with the knife. Before he had a chance to plunge the blade at my hand, I caught the wrist of his armed hand. I then used my other hand to punch his arm. Jacob groaned and dropped the knife but I caught the knife with my free hand. I tackled Jacob to the ground, brought his arm across his chest and brought the knife to his throat. I was on top of him before I even realized what had just happened. I just overpowered Jacob! I let go of Jacob's arm and stood up.

"You see," said Sylfano as she helped bring up Jacob, "you have some skills within you. When you became a dragon, you learned, I mean, you developed fighting skills instantly."

"That was an incredible experience," I said. "I never really knew what was going on or what I was doing until the last second."

Jacob replied, "All your actions were part of your reflex. It is not an ability sort to say, but dragons have their reflexes enhanced, so when a surprise attack happens to them, let's say being ambushed, the dragons are prepared for a fight. They will know what to do when it comes to hand to hand combat. However, gargoyles can also attack from the sky using very powerful sound waves called crushing waves. The crushing waves can destroy anything in its path. Even with your strong skin, you could still be hurt by the crushing waves. Those waves will cut your skin open like a blade wound, so it would be wise to avoid the crushing waves. These crushing waves can be seen only to dragons and dragon-lords since we all share the dragon's sight. There is also another attack that the gargoyles use. It is called the wave of discord. This attack explodes on impact."

"That's all great information," Jamano said, "but how will Dracollus defend himself against gargoyles when they are in the air using their crushing wave? He can't always be dodging their attacks; he needs to know some offensive attack to use at the gargoyles, especially if the gargoyles are attacking Dracollus from the air."

"THAT," Sylfano said, "is what we are trying to teach him now with these fire lessons. First thing for us to do is make you learn the different ways of using your pyrokinesis.”

“The first type of pyrokinesis is the flamethrower ability,” Jacob said. “The flamethrower ability is the easiest of the pyrokinesis there is. You use your fire like a flamethrower.”

“Let me show you,” Sylfano said.

Sylfano held out her hand as if she was trying to stop someone. Then fire just shot out from her hand and the flames blew about five krompus away from where she was standing. The fire lasted for about a minute and then died out. Sylfano put her hand down.

“That is what the flamethrower ability looks like,” she said casually as if she does it all the time. “As Jacob said before it is the easiest ability to do and master. Let’s see if you can do it. Here, let me help you.”

She took the knife from my hand and tried to position my hand properly.

“Now concentrate on summoning some fire from your hand,” she told me.

I tried to summon some fire from my hand, but I was more concentrated on Sylfano’s hand touching my arm. Her smooth skin was so gentle on my skin. All I could concentrate on was how her skin was warming my arm. The slightest pressure from her hand on my arm made my entire body shiver.

“I can’t summon any fire with you holding my arm,” I told her. “You’re distracting me.”

"In the world outside of Housay," Jacob said, "there will be a lot of things that will distract you thanks to your enhanced senses. You have already learned how to block some noises out of the way. This would be a good lesson on how to block out some other distractions."

"Can we please do it some other time?" I begged, "Because the only thing I can think of is how soft your skin is on my arm."

"You will just have to get used to it then," she said, "since I will put both my hands on your arm, and that will make you even more distracted. Summon some fire from your hand or I will."

"Ok," I snapped, "I get the picture. Now let me try and concentrate."

Trying to summon fire would have been easier if Sylfano was not distracting me, but I couldn't ignore a valuable lesson. So, I tried to imagine fire coming out of my hand while still thinking about Sylfano. Nothing happened. This time I willed the fire to shoot out from my hand. Still, nothing happened. I was just about to give up when Sylfano put her second hand on my arm. That got my full attention. Now all I could think about was how her hands were on my arm. They felt like they belonged there. Her warm and radiating touch was driving my mind blank. Nothing in the world would be able to knock me out of how I was feeling.

"Now try and do it again," Sylfano said. "And this time, try not to think about me."

Now I could no longer resist not looking at her. I turned my head to look at her. Her eyes were beautiful looking straight at me. Looking into them mesmerized me. I could not stop looking at her reptilian green eyes as they looked back at me. Her true beauty emanated; she was perfect just the way she was. Her mouth was open just a little bit to show a tiny bit of her front teeth.

After staring at her for a few seconds, fire shot out from my hand. The flames shot across ten krompus away from me. It died after a few seconds. That's when Sylfano let go of my arm and applauded for me. Everybody then applauded for me.

"That was great, Dracollus! Keep up the good work!"

"I really don't know how I summoned that flamethrower," I said. "All I could literally think about was you, Sylfano."

"You'll know the answer to that when you start working on the next lesson of fire," Jacob said, "and that would be the fireball. Now I know the fireball looks easy to do, but it's not. It is extremely hard."

"You may know how to summon fire," Sylfano said, "but now controlling the fire you summon and make sure it hits its target, IS the hard part!"

"Controlling fire doesn't sound that difficult to do," I said confidently.

"Well, it is. Now follow me."

She marched ahead of me. We all followed her all the way to where she was leading us, to the parking lot of the nuclear power plant. She made us stop in the middle of the parking lot. She turned towards me and said,

"Now this is where we will be getting you started on throwing a fireball. First I want you to throw a fireball at that transport." She pointed to one of the transports that were in bad condition. This transport had the front mashed up as if it had crashed into a wall. The hood was crumpled and the left headlight was partly dangling. This transport also had some cracks over its front windshield, as if someone had been trying to break the windshield open with a bat.

"I want you to use your fireball to blow up that transport. Now don't worry if you can't get it the first time."

"What's so wrong with this?"

I thrust my hand towards the transport while thinking about Sylfano, and shot a column of fire towards the transport instantly torching it. The transport was on fire. Then, it exploded, shot up ten krompus into the air, and landed with a loud crash. I looked towards Sylfano and she slapped in my face.

"That is not what I asked you to do!" Sylfano snapped, "Now we have to end lessons for the day because of your little stunt. We want your lessons to be done as quickly and as quietly as possible." Then she ran away, with Jacob running behind her. The rest of us went to our respective homes.

■ ■

The next day, we all came back to the power plant. The transport that was on fire was now charred but no longer in flames.

"Now THIS time I want you to hurl a fireball like this." She opened her palm and a fireball came to life in her hand. She then hurled the fire towards a transport, and the fire hit the rear transport door. The fire only hit the transport, but the transport did not catch.

"That is what I want you to do," she said angrily, "Now try and do it without making so much destruction."

"Ok," I said dumbly. "I'll do it."

"Wait! Before you do that, drink some of this."

She reached into her pocket and handed me a small flask. I opened the flask and took a swig, only to recoil at the taste of the liquid inside the flask. It was so BITTER! It was like drinking some liquid blish! (Blish is what you call manure as a curse) I spat all of it out.

"What the Helmam is this stuff?" I asked. "It tastes so disgusting!"

"That is igniter fluid," Sylfano said "this will help you have more firepower. Now finish what's left of the igniter fluid."

I didn't want anymore, but I did what she told me to do. As the liquid traveled down my throat, I could literally feel how awful it was going down. I was pretty sure that if my face was any tighter you could no longer see any part of my eyes or nose. It was as if my face was completely blank. After I finished the igniter fluid, I tossed aside the flask. I spat on the ground to try and get rid of some of the awful taste that was in my mouth. After the taste of the lighter fluid was gone from my mouth (which took about half an hour), I looked at the transport. I opened my palm and brought some fire to my hand. I tried to let the fire sail towards the transport, but the fire was stuck to my hand. I tried to throw it away, but nothing happened.

"Ok, WHY is the fire stuck to my hand?" I asked urgently.

"That's because you're not doing it right," Jacob said. "You have to imagine the fire hitting its target."

"But that is only the beginning of the problem," Sylfano added. "When you throw your fireball towards the transport, your fire will extinguish. You need to know how to control your fire when it is sailing in midair."

"Ok," I replied.

I got started trying to imagine that my fire would only hit the transport and not cause it to catch fire. I then threw the fire at the transport, only for the fire to be extinguished in midair. I tried once more and again it did not work. I kept trying to hit the transport for an hour and still nothing. My fireballs were nowhere even close to hitting the transport. I knew that I could do it if I was closer, but I also knew that Sylfano and Jacob wanted me to do it from a good distance.

"What gives?" I asked. "How do I try and control my fire?"

"Oh yeah, I forgot to mention that," Jacob said, "The easiest way for you to control your fire is to experiencing some form of emotion. You need a strong emotion to let go of the fire that is on you. The stronger the emotion is, the more in control you will be of your fire. Since you're calm, the fire doesn't go that far. The strongest emotion is rage just for your information."

"Ok, now you tell me," I said annoyed.

"That's good," said Sylfano, "You can use that annoyance to control your fire."

"Thanks for the info," I said sarcastically.

I felt a little rage building up, and then I threw my fireball at the transport. The fireball made a big dent in the transport's rear side, and then it went out.

"That was good, Dracollus, but can you hit smaller targets?" she quipped, bursting my bubble.

Chapter 9

An Unusual Power

Sylfano brought me to the side of the power plant where there were several empty tin cans on the walkway path. All the cans were charred as if Sylfano had already used them for target practice. The cans were in a straight line horizontally.

"Now let us see if you can hit these targets from here," she dared.

We were about 50 krompus away from the cans so it was a good spot to test my aim.

"Now this time, when you use your fireball, I want you to use a small fireball like this..."
She summoned a fireball that was the size of a candle flame, and then she hurled it towards the can that was closest to her. She hit the can dead center and it got knocked over.

"Now, you try."

"But how do I even make such a small fire?" I protested.

"The way to do that is to have the courage to summon a small fire." She winked as if she just told a joke.

I tried to will my fire to be the size of a candle flame, but the fireball that came out was the size of a baseball. I tried to make my fire smaller by decreasing the amount I had but all that did was make the fire go out. I tried again, but this time, nothing happened. I wondered what Sylfano meant when she said that I needed the courage to summon a small fire. And then it hit me. She meant to say that I needed to believe that I could summon a small flame, so I tried to believe that my fire was small and that I could do it. At that instant, my flame decreased its size to a small candle flame.

"Cool!" I muttered.

Suddenly the flame went back to being the size of a baseball.

"Oops. I guess that I really need to concentrate on believing in myself while I try and shoot small flames. Speaking of which, why do I even need to summon small flames?"

"You don't really need it as an offensive weapon," Jacob said, "but having to use a small flame makes it easier when you need to put out the fire."

"Sometimes, dragons need to put out the fire that they have started," Sylfano said. "We believe that those who are not involved with our war should not have to suffer from our battles. Therefore, they should not have to be hurt by our flames. We try to minimize the amount of damage to the innocent. It is the enemy that must sustain the most damage."

"OK," I said, nodding.

I concentrated on believing that I could make a small flame. That's when my fire started to compress until my flame was the size of a candle flame. Next, I willed myself to believe that my flame could hit the can furthest can away from me. It took a lot of focused thinking. I also summoned my strength to hurl my fire. I missed the first time. I tried it again, and this time, I hit my target in the dead center and knocked it over. I did it repeatedly until I hit all the cans. I would miss every now and then, but eventually, I hit all of them.

"That was perfect!" Sylfano said. "Now let's see if you can fire small flames without any shrinking. In other words; summon a small flame. Haruasore set the cans up again please"

"Why do I have to be the one to do that?" he complained.

"Because you're a dragon-lord and dragon-lords are supposed to help train dragons, and you haven't helped train Dracollus yet, so do yourself and Dracollus a favor by setting up the cans on those barrels."

"Alright, fine," he muttered.

He went over to the cans but instead of putting them up where they were previously stationed, he put them even farther away from us. He then walked over to us.

"I hope it's OK that I put them even farther away," he said when he returned.

"That's more than OK. That's perfect," said Jamano. "Now Dracollus can test his aim and accuracy even more."

"That is absolutely correct." Sylfano said skeptically, "In fact, those were the words I was going to say; word for word. How did you know that?"

"Oh, uh" Jamano hesitated before finally responding, "I don't how I knew that."

"OK, anyway moving on," Sylfano said, "Now Dracollus can you-" She was cut off by me.

I felt like there was a sneeze coming out of my nose (which is very strange because I have never sneezed in my entire life). I was on my way to "Achoo!"

"AAA. AAAH. AAH"

"EVERYBODY DUCK FOR COVER!" Sylfano yelled, "HE'S GONNA BLOW."

Sylfano disappeared with Jacob Mas Pal, while Jamano ran and hid behind an oil drum, and Haruasore stopped coming towards me then turned to his left, ran, and hid behind a partially destroyed wall of a building on my right side. I sneezed. When I sneezed, an icicle shot out from my mouth piercing a tin can dead center. It took me a while to realize that my dream had just come true. That got me worried because if this dream came true, then that would mean that my DEATH was coming up.

A few minutes after I sneezed everyone emerged from his or her hiding place. Sylfano reappeared from next to me with a trail of dust coming from her side. Jacob came in from behind.

"That is what is what we were hiding from." Jamano asked, "I thought that Dracollus was going to blow up and not just shoot that…that…whatever it is."

"Incredible," Sylfano said. "I had hoped that this new power of yours would not have appeared so soon."

"And what power is that?" I asked.

"This power of yours is to create ice."

"Are you kidding me?" Haruasore said with a smile. "Do you know how rare that power is, Sylfano?"

"Of course I know, Haruasore - I am the Princess of the Ancient Dragons, remember?"

"Oops," Haruasore said dumbly while he slapped himself in the forehead. "I forgot. But you have to admit, this is a really exciting thing."

"WHOA. WHOA. Wait a minute," I said, using my arms to calm down everyone down. "Can someone please explain to me properly what this new ability of mine is?"

Haruasore turned towards Sylfano.

"May I please explain to Dracollus everything on this new ability, your Highness?" he asked her. "It's kind of my specialty."

"Since when are you an expert on the ice ability?" Sylfano asked him.

"My great-great-grandfather was a trainer of an ice dragon. He taught that dragon how to use her ice abilities. The knowledge of training a dragon to use ice has been passed from generation to generation ever since. I am the only who knows how to train Dracollus. Besides, you said I should help train Dracollus, and this is the way for me to help train him."

"All right, then," she said to him.

He turned towards me.

"Ice bending is a rare ability that only certain dragons can do. They are very rare in this part of the Helmamnor. Not only are they master of controlling fire, but they are also masters of manipulating water. Now that you have unlocked this ability, you will no longer be affected by water. You can drink water again with no harm."

"Can we please get to the part on how I use this ice power?" I asked impatiently.

"I'm getting to that part," Haruasore reassured me. "But now listen to what I have to say. Bending water is tricky, but creating ice is easy. All you must do is concentrate on making the air around a certain thing be cold. Once you do that, the air will become ice. Why don't you try that out with those cans?"

"Before I even do anything can someone please explain to me why I have this ability or power to make ice appear?"

"No one really knows how this power is acquired," Jacob explained. "The only dragons that are able to do this power are the Dragons of the Water and the Magical Dragons. Judging from all that I have seen from you, I am guessing that you are most likely a member of either the Magical Dragons or the Ancient Dragons. You are most like a Magical Dragon because of your new powers, possibly even both, but there is no way that you are a Dragon of the Water. Now get BACK to your training!"

"OK…"

I tried to imagine that the air around the can was cold and that it would turn to ice. Nothing happened.

"Nothing's happening." I said, "What am I doing wrong?"

"Oh, silly me." Haruasore said, "I forgot to let you know that it is easier if some part of your body was pointed at an object. Use your hands to guide your ability to know what it is you want to freeze."

"Thanks, Haruasore. You could have told me that earlier." I sighed in disbelief.

I pointed my finger to a specific tin can, the closest one to me. I tried again, and this time, a breeze came from my finger to the can and ice formed on the can. When the can was completely frozen I put my hand down.

"That was great, Dracollus!" Haruasore said. "Now try and make ice appear above the cans. That will be a little more of a challenge."

"Alright," I said. "I'll take the challenge."

I held my hand out and aimed it above the next can. I concentrated on making the air above the can turn to ice. Nothing happened at first. I tried again, and this time, I willed the temperature in the air to decrease so that it could transform into ice. There came another breeze from my hand and ice formed above the can.

When I put my hand down the ice fell on top of the can, crushing the can instantly and breaking the ice.

"That was awesome. Now here comes the tricky part. It's time for you to learn how to manipulate water."

He took out a bottle of water and twisted the top off.

"Alright, this time, I want you to lift the water out of its container. Go ahead and try," he said encouraging me.

"Ok."

I concentrated on moving the water out of its container. The water did not budge. I used my hand to help guide my powers. I lifted my arm up and pointed my hand towards the container and tried once more. Still, nothing happened even after a minute of holding my arm out.

"It's not moving," I said, dropping my tired arm.

"Why don't you close your eyes?" Jamano suggested. "That will help you concentrate more. If anything happens, I'll let you know."

"That sounds like a good idea."

"Of course it's a good idea," Haruasore said, "since it's coming from my girlfriend. So you Dracollus better do it, or you will never know the limits of using your ice powers."

"OK. OK. You don't have to be all bossy."

I lifted my arm once more, and this time, I closed my eyes in concentration. I imagined that the water would exit the top and leave not a single drop in the container. When no one said anything, I opened my eyes. The water was just in its container. Nothing had happened. I tried once more closing my eyes. Now this time, I imagined the water was obeying my command, and it was exiting its container. I felt like I could command the water in the container. All of a sudden, there was a tingly feeling in my arm. There was a cold feeling through my arm, and when I opened my eyes, I saw that the water was beginning to exit the bottle as if it was being sucked out. The water hovered a few willmers above the bottle. The water looked like it was in a puddle in midair. When the bottle was empty, I turned my hand over, and then flexed my hand. The water followed my motions.

"You did it!" Jamano said as she hugged me. That broke my concentration, and the water spilled to the ground.

"Thanks, Jamano," I said, "You made me lose my concentration."

"Oops," she replied, "Sorry."

"That was some good work Dracollus." Sylfano said, "I think that is enough excitement and enough training for the day. Why don't you all come back at ten o'clock tomorrow? Then we can reset the place for Dracollus to practice his ice bending skills."

Chapter 10

A Bigger Terror

"This is incredible news, Dracollus!" my mother exclaimed after I showed her and father my ice ability. "This proves that you could be the dragon that we have been waiting for."

"Uh honey-" my father said started to say before I interrupted him.

"What dragon is that?" I asked.

My mother put her hand over her mouth and widened her eyes as if she let out something that she was not supposed to say.

"Uh well, Dracollus," my father said, "that is something we should not talk about."

"No," my mother said as she put her hand down and readjusted her eyes, "We should talk about this. He has a right to know. After all, he could be the one who ends all of our struggles."

"Well," my father said while thinking. After a while of thinking, he said, "Alright. The evidence is piling up and there is a chance that he is the one."

"I am the one of what?" I asked.

"Thousands of years ago," my mother said, "The old dragon prophet, the father of the current one, said that one dragon and one gargoyle shall work together to end this war. The dragons and Helmams have been waiting patiently for that one dragon to come, but so far we yet to witness the prophecy close to being fulfilled.”

“We have reason to believe that you are the Dragon Bringer,” my father said.

“What’s a Dragon Bringer?” I asked. “And what makes you think I’m one?”

“It’s not what a Dragon Bringer is,” my father said “it’s WHO the Dragon Bringer is. You will know more when you hear the prophecy.”

“What prophecy?”

“The prophecy was given the day that the Former Dragon Prophet had foreseen the end of the war. In the prophecy, it gives a vague meaning of what the future holds for everyone on this planet. Everyone on the planet knows the name of the prophecy but few know what the prophecy says. The prophecy is called The Bringer’s Prophecy.”

“May I know more about the prophecy?”

“Now THAT,” my mother said, “is something that you must ask Sylfano for. We are forbidden to speak the prophecy, or even write it down.”

“Why is that?” I inquired further. “Why is it forbidden for you guys to speak or write the prophecy?”

“Most of the people here in Housay don’t know the ways of magic. The people who know the prophecy are mostly either dragons or sorcerers. Most likely sorcerers since there are very few dragons in Housay.”

"Why is it forbidden for you to even talk about it?" I asked. "I mean, it is not like anyone is listening right now!"

"Well that is the thing," my mother said, "You never know who is actually listening to us right now."

"Well enough chitchat," my father said, "You should get some rest and find out more about your future. You never know what could happen or what is happening depending on what you dream about."

I looked out the kitchen window. The sun was starting to set, but tomorrow night was the full moon. This is the only time this month that I can train myself before the full moon when I was at my strongest at night. Besides, I had yet to be trained at night. All the training that I had done throughout the course was done during the day. I was hoping that I could go somewhere to have some nighttime training, and I knew just the place and person to go to.

"I'll go to sleep later," I told my parents. "Right now I want to have a word with Sylfano."

"What's wrong?" my mother asked.

"Oh, nothing," I said, "I just want to talk to her. I'll be out for an hour or two depending on how much I need to tell her and how much she needs to tell me."

"What do you need to talk to her about?" my father asked.

"After our conversation, I think it's pretty obvious." I pointed out.

"Oh," My father said. "Well, why don't you do that in the morning?"

"I know," I replied, "but right now I'm restless and I want to hear the rest of the reasons why you think that I am the Bringer of the Dragons. I'll be back as soon as I can. See you later." I exited the house.

I ran towards Sylfano's house using the same routine I did to drive her home on our date night. I used my speed to get there faster. If anybody was on the road, all they would see was a blur. I was that blur of course. When I got there, the sun was setting. I knocked on the door. I waited a few seconds until Jacob answered the door.

"Dracollus!" he said. "What a surprise to see you here."

"Hello, Jacob." I said, "I'm here to see Sylfano. Is she available to talk?"

"Sylfano is not available to talk right now."

"Why not?" I asked.

"Who's at the door Jacob," Sylfano asked behind Jacob.

She came in my line of sight behind Jacob at the door. She was wearing a dark blue robe with golden dragons on it. The robe she was wearing was very shiny like the fabric was literally reflecting the different colors of light. While Sylfano was wearing that elegant robe, she looked kind of… well… sexy… I guess. I couldn't help but stare at her. "Hello, Dracollus," she said to me. "What brings you here to my house at this time?" She didn't seem to notice that I was staring at her with great awe.

"Uh," I said to her. "I was wondering if we could talk. That is, of course, if you are not busy right now."

"I'm not busy - we can talk. Come on in. I'll just put on some clothes and then we can talk. I'll meet you in the living room." With that, she left to go change out of her robe.

I entered the house and went into the living room. I could wander around the house for hours and weeks, but I would always have some awe for the living room. I kept walking around the room looking at different paintings on the wall this time. One painting seemed to catch my attention today. I saw this painting when I first saw her living room, but now I was more focused on it. The painting depicted a dragon being surrounded by gargoyles on the ground. Above the dragon, there was what looked like a winged man. The winged man had wings like an owl. Dark brown feathers were sprouting out from behind him. The man had a sword in his left hand that was shining blue. I keep wondering why most blades I see are made of shiny blue. I was still looking at the painting for a few minutes when Sylfano came into the living room wearing a green Shirt and a dark gray skirt.

"So what is it you wanted to talk about?" she asked me.

"Well," I paused to collect my thoughts, "my parents told me of their opinion about why I have such special gifts. They think that I am the Bringer of the Dragons."

Sylfano's eyebrows formed closely together. "Do you even know what that means?" she asked inquisitively.

"My parents told me what the Bringer is as best as they could without telling me the prophecy. Apparently, the Bringer is supposed to work with a gargoyle to end this war. At least that is what they told me."

"They were correct, but there is more to the story."

"Can you tell me what the prophecy is?"

Sylfano smiled but had a sad look in her eyes. "When the time is right, I will tell you what the prophecy is. You are still a young dragon who still has a lot of training to do."

"But my parents think that I could be the Bringer of the Dragons."

"My parents thought I was the Bringer of the Dragons, too, until I was defeated by an Ancient Gargoyle four hundred and three years ago. I was humiliated by that battle. That battle was one of the many reasons why I had to leave the kingdom. I learned after being away from the kingdom for about a century that I was a little impulsive at that time, so when I say that you should wait because you are still a novice, I also mean that you need to be patient."

She put her hand on my shoulder. At that moment I was feeling very dizzy, then everything went black.

■■■

When I could see clearly again, I knew that what I was seeing was a dream. At the beginning of my dream, I saw different flocks of gargoyles at the border wall of Housay, the West side of the border by the looks of it (that side is where the gargoyles rule). The walls are twenty krompus high, but per the legend of the walls, they are protected by magic that can reach the entire sky. Onc dclta gargoyle tried to fly over the wall, but as soon as it reached the end section of the wall closest to Housay (that would be the Industrial District) an invisible barrier became visible with showing shades of green shimmered. When the gargoyle hit the barrier that gargoyle became a stream of mist. The other gargoyles just flew in place for a while. It was as if they were waiting for something to happen. After about a few more minutes of waiting, the green barrier showed itself. A second later it, shattered. The green shards of the barrier disappeared the next second after the barrier had been destroyed. Another gargoyle had gone ahead of the flock and flown straight into the Industrial District. Then, all the gargoyles flew into Housay. All the flocks went into the different district of Housay. I saw what the gargoyles were doing in every district they were in. They attacked people in the district; some shot out disks of green light while others were biting people.

Skipping ahead of all the carnage and destruction I saw in my dream there was this one scene that I could not believe I was seeing. I saw a building on fire from the Industrial District that looked very familiar. The building was missing a section of the wall, and it was on the road. Three gargoyles were shooting shiny green things at the building. Apparently, they were trying to destroy the building. I was wondering exactly how they got past the defenses of Housay. I then looked down to the streets. There were piles of debris all over the streets, and some bodies lying lifelessly. Someone was trapped underneath the part of the wall that had fallen to the road. The building was about to crumble on top of the person that was trapped, and I realized that person was Sylfano! I was witnessing her death. Or at least when I was having this dream I thought it was her death that I was seeing. I could see the building fall slowly. Then quickly, the building started to increase its speed in falling. After a few more seconds, I was sure that Sylfano was going to be crushed by this building!!

The scene then changed to the same room that is filled with fire. Only this time, the dragon was not around. I moved towards the back of the room to see if the dragon was there. The dragon was not there. Suddenly the fire went out and the room became dark.

After what seemed like a few minutes there was a light at the other end of the room. I moved towards the light and saw the red dragon was at the entrance of the room. The dragon said to me transpathically in Jarcannoph,

"You have returned. I was beginning to wonder if you would ever return."

"Who are you, oh great powerful dragon? And why do you look so familiar to me?"

"At this time, you don't need to know who I am. As to why I look familiar to you, I don't know. We have never fully met. You saw me only once when you were a baby and that was when I was in my human form."

"We met before?" I asked skeptically. And then it hit me. "You're my father!"

"Yes, Dracollus. I am your father."

"How are we even communicating through a dream, or better yet, why am I here?"

"I brought you here. It is the only way I know how to communicate with you. In the dream world, I can communicate with you. Although I cannot see you, it is good to hear your voice and feel your presence. I am very far away from you, Dracollus. I have missed you."

"You MISS me. How could you even miss me? You're the one that sent me to Lunfa and Ilsa. Why did you even send me to them, and most importantly why can't I know who you are, right now?"

"That will be answered in the future."

"WHY CAN'T YOU JUST TELL ME NOW?" I asked impatiently.

"You are not yet ready to know who I am, my son. If you were to find out who I am, your destiny will be corrupted. Now, wake up my son. You still have to complete your training. Please don't mention any of this to your friends and Lunfa, for if they find out, all that I have done to hide you will be for nothing."

"You hid me? Why?"

He waved his hand/paw as if he was saying goodbye.

I woke up. I sat up straight gasping for air. I was in a bed, but I don't know whose bed I was in.

"DRACOLLUS!" a voice beseeched. "You're awake!"

I turned around to see that Sylfano, Jacob, Haruasore, Jamano, and my parents were all in the room.

"What just happened?" I asked.

"You tell us!" Sylfano said, "When I put my hand on your shoulder, you passed out. At first, I thought you had fainted, but then I heard you snoring."

"Her Highness and I," Jacob said softly, "assumed you were asleep, but you have been asleep for 41 hours. That's more than a day, you know."

"ASLEEP?" I asked. "Then what are all of you guys doing here?"

"We all got worried that you might be cursed or something," my mother said. "That's why we are all here."

"Well, you guys should not worry about me. You should worry more about Sylfano."

"What is there for all of us to worry about me?" she asked.

I told them all about the dream that I just had and the one I had about an invasion about to happen in Housay. They were all shocked. I didn't want to tell them about the dream I had with my father. As much as I really wanted to tell everyone about that dream, from what my father had said, maybe that was not such a good idea.

"Dracollus," my father Lunfa said, "You should have told us about this invasion. IF there is an invasion about to happen, we have to warn the elder guardians."

"They are already on alert for an invasion," Jacob said.

"How?" Jamano asked. "We only found out about this now."

"You may have found out about the invasion just now," Sylfano said, "but we have known about a planned invasion since Dracollus' birthday."

"How did you know that?" we asked Sylfano and Jacob.

"We knew there was an invasion the minute you stopped terrorizing the Ancient District," Jacob said.

"After I shot you down from the sky," Sylfano said taking over, "there was a flash of lighting in the sky. All the smoke cleared from the sky instantly, and there was a symbol in the sky. That symbol represented destruction in the ancient language of the gargoyles. Now, since you had just attacked the place, I knew that there was either a spy in Housay and that person knew that there was an attack here, or that there will be an invasion that's about to happen soon. After a few cycles of discussion behind your backs, I'm sorry for us to do that, we decided that the symbol meant both. I knew the invasion was going to happen because the all of the gargoyles want me dead, and now since I am here they will work to accomplish that. That had been the gargoyles' plan since I left the Ancient Dragon Kingdom."

"Why did you come here then?" Jamano asked.

"My parents and I agreed that it was best for me to stay hidden until the time was right. We thought that this was the safest place to be. But when we found out there was a spy I knew that I was in danger."

"So why did you stay and not run away?" I asked her.

"I had no choice. Even if I did run away, this place would still be attacked, and you're your lack of experience or training, you would surely get killed.

Besides if I ran away, the gargoyles would find me before I got back to my palace and kill me."

Everyone was silent for a while, then I said, "Alright then, I should get back to training."

"What? NO!" my father said. "That is a bad idea because you are in no condition to re-start training."

"I slept for 41 hours, dad. I am well-rested, and I need to complete my training if I am going to stand a chance against the gargoyles when they attack."

"Dracollus is right," Sylfano opined, "He needs to complete his training, and this is the best time to test his ability to fly at night."

Chapter 11

Across the Night Sky

My parents went home to the Middle district while Jamano and Haruasore stayed behind. Sylfano said that they should get some rest, but they both wanted to see me transform again.

"Before he does that," Jacob said. "He needs to warm up first. I know, I know - he can do it without warming up, but it is still better for him to do it. After all, getting all that adrenaline to the heart can make the changing process easier."

"Alright, so what do you want me to do?" I asked.

"Well, first of all, you can start by running to your house and coming back here." Sylfano said, "That should be a good warm-up for you to do."

"Alright, but is it OK…"

"Yes, Dracollus," Sylfano cut me off, "You can use your super speed to make things faster."

"OK, so I'll see you guys in a couple of minutes."

I ran towards my house, taking a longer route. Instead of going to the main road, I used the walkway bridge to get to my house. I got there in a matter of minutes and stopped to catch my breath a little. I was a little tired; after all, I had just woken up from 41 hours of sleeping, and this was the first exercise I had done today/this evening. Correction, this is the first exercise

I have done ALL day. I waited a few minutes until I had gotten my breathing steady, and then I started to run back to Sylfano's house. I used the same route I did to get from her house to my house.

When I got to her house, no one was there anymore. I went to the backyard and still, nobody was there. That's when I sensed something coming from behind me. I turned around just in time to see that a gallon of water was headed towards me. I used my ice bending powers to freeze the water in its tracks. I watched as the water, turned to ice, fell to the ground and shattered into pieces. I looked up and saw that Sylfano was carrying an empty bucket.

"That was good, Dracollus," she said. "I thought that your ability to sense danger would be dull, but clearly it is not."

"Where are Jamano and Haruasore?" I asked

"They are with Jacob on their way to the Forest District."

"Why are they headed to that district? It's all the way on the other side of Housay."

"Yes, that is correct. We thought that it would be a good idea for them to catch some rest while you are practicing flying."

"Oh, that's actually a good idea."

"Anyway," she said, "let's see you transform again."

I closed my eyes in concentration. I willed my body to change into a dragon. There was a feeling inside of me that seemed like all my organs inside my body were going to explode. I guess I will always have to experience this feeling every time I transform. I opened my eyes to see that my mouth had stretched into a snout, and within a couple of seconds I completed my transformation. I looked at Sylfano and saw that she had transformed into her dragon form. Looking at her properly now, she was gorgeous. Her scales were purple; her wings were covered in scales unlike mine; she had beautiful golden eyes; blue spikes on her back that were about a foot long, her dragon face was long and gorgeous, two black horns the shape of large spikes were just inches away from her long pointed ears that… oh, sorry. I got carried away again.

Back to the story, I realized that Sylfano was wearing an emerald crown, with rubies embedded in it, on her head. The crown was not there in her human form, so I asked her, "How did you get that crown on your head? It wasn't there before you were human."

"You're right, Dracollus," she said, "It was not on my head at the beginning. When I transform into my dragon form, this crown is summoned to my head to indicate that I am the princess of the ancient dragons."

"That kind of gives you away to the enemy if you think about it."

"Not really," she replied, "For you see, only dragons can see the crown of a royal dragon, and gargoyles cannot see the crown."

"How is that possible?"

"The crown is enchanted with magic," she said, making it sound obvious.

"Oh, right."

"But enough talk. Let's see you take flight."

With that, she lifted her wings from her side and flapped them, causing her to be lifted from the ground and make wind part the ground a little. I looked at my wings before I flapped them as well. Flapping my wings was even easier than I had thought. The wings on my back felt like arms, and my front legs (which were my actual arms I should point out) felt like actual legs. After flapping my wings for a few seconds, I rose about a good few yards above the ground. I continued to flap them until Sylfano said to me transpathically, "STOP!"

I looked down to see that she was still close to the ground, while I was already as high as her roof, which meant that I was flying three stories high.

"Sylfano, what are you doing down there?" I inquired.

"What are you doing up there?" she bellowed

"I thought we were supposed to be flying. Why are you flying so low?"

"We are supposed to keep a low profile. Can you please come down here?"

"Alright," I said as I lowered myself to her level.

"Now, follow me into the woods and try not to cause so much attention."

She flew into the woods behind her backyard. I followed. My wings could just barely dodge the trees in the woods. The trees in these woods were well spaced out for a dragon to fly into. I think that was maybe the point. Sylfano told me, "This is where we will fly."

With that, she flew into the sky. I caught up with her within seconds of flying through the sky. I felt a sense of freedom as I flew through the sky. People of Housay were never allowed to fly using airplanes or helicopters. It was forbidden thanks to the war of the dragons and gargoyles. Only on one special event, which is the day that Housay was created, would there be the use of airplanes and helicopters. Unfortunately for me, only the people of the rich district could get a chance to ride in such things. I wondered if Sylfano had a chance to ride a helicopter.

"No, Dracollus," a voice said to me in my head that just suddenly appeared. "I never did."

"Hmm," I replied.

"I read your mind, Dracollus," Sylfano said transpathically, "and I answered your question. Besides, why would I fly in an airplane if I can fly right now?"

"Oh, right," I transpathically said dumbly.

"It's alright. Flying for the first time can cause some distractions to dragons. I know it did to me. I lost sight of my father during my first time flying. Just like you have right now."

"What do you mean?"

It was only then that I realized that Sylfano was no longer in front of me. I looked in every direction to find her and found out that she was right beside me on my left.

"Don't let distraction get the better of you. That was what we have been training you to do along. NOW let us do some real flying lessons."

She then went ahead of me.

"First let us see if you can dive," she said, "Follow me."

She pointed her nose to the ground, turn her body towards the ground, and let her wings rest on her side before she finally dove for the ground. I copied her and dove for the ground. About a minute of diving, she spread her wings out and flapped them making her stay in place. I did the same thing with my wings and caught myself flying in place.

"That's great Dracollus!" Sylfano said in my mind again.

"Why are we speaking transpathically?" I asked.

"Because we would have to yell to hear each other, that's why."

"Why would we have to yell?"

"Do you think you could hear me at this kind of altitude?"

"Oh, right."

"Anyway, we should head to the meeting place."

"What meeting place?"

"The place where we will meet Jacob and your friends. Let's go"

"Why are we going there so soon?"

"Because the sun is going to be coming up soon, and we don't want any people to know that there are dragons in Housay now, would we?"

I thought about it for a second to understand what she meant, and then I understood. "Alright, let's go."

We arrived at the meeting spot just in time, too. The sun was beginning to rise. The gang was not yet there, so we waited. The place where we were supposed to meet was a clearing in the middle of the Forest District. Local hunters called this area The Iris because if you were to look from above the section, it would look exactly like the iris of the eye. In the center of the circle was a tree, the oldest tree here in the Forest District. That is where I am pacing right now. The tree is about seventy krompus tall and was about seventeen krompus wide.

"Jacob can sometimes arrive late to a place," Sylfano said, trying to reassure me. We had been waiting for about an hour now. "Especially if he is with someone."

"That can happen I guess, but what could they be doing that is…"

I stopped because I sensed something. Something that was not right, yet it felt very familiar. I turned around to see someone come out of the woods. It was not Jacob that came out of the woods, nor any of my friends….

It was Pireluve.

Chapter 12

A Dark Past

Before I continue with the story, I think it's about time I tell you about my past with Pireluve. When we were kids, we were best friends. I think I was about four years old when I met him. Bear in mind this was long before I met Jamano and Haruasore. As a little child, Pireluve loved to cause all kinds of mischief. We used to pull pranks on other kids; just pranks, no bullying. Some people called us the 'Duo Pranksters'. Everybody had a great laugh when we pulled a prank on them. Sometimes, I yearn for those old cycles.

Back then, my parents always told me that Pireluve was a bad person to be with. I just ignored what they had to say and continued to be with my friend. I had a great time with Pireluve during my early childhood, but then things changed. It was like Pireluve had become sinister overnight. Now that I think about it, it was probably more like within a week that he changed. I asked him what had happened to him. The only thing that he would ever tell me was 'I know who I really am', or 'I know what my destiny is now'. Afterward, he wanted to do bigger pranks on people. Not just kids, but teenager and adults as well. At first, they were fun to do but after doing the bigger pranks for a while, I started to hate them. Some kids ended up crying after our pranks. I felt sorry for them after a while. I tried to end the big pranks with Pireluve and go back to doing small pranks. Unfortunately, all he said to me was, "We need to do this, it is our purpose of living, you idiot. If you don't want to continue, then you are not my friend anymore, and you will be the person I will forever hate the most."

I wanted to be his friend and not be hated by him so I continued the pranks, although the more I continued, the more I felt ashamed of myself. I was losing who I was the longer I kept spending time with Pireluve. I would only do more pranks until this one time when we pulled a prank on this girl. It was this one prank that made me not only end my friendship with Pireluve but change my entire life forever. I was about eight years old when I did the last prank with Pireluve. We were going to scare the girl with a large spider. This girl was very afraid of spiders at the time. We caught a spider that was the size of a pencil end. We put it in a box to show the girl. We found her by the docks of the lake that is in the Middle District. She looked as if she was waiting for someone. We approached her and said hi.

"Hello," the girl said, "What's in that box you are holding?"

"The box is for you," Pireluve said.

"Would you like to see what is in it?" I asked.

"Is this a prank?" she asked suspiciously as she crossed her arms.

"No, this is a peace offering," I said, "for the prank, we did to you earlier. We, I mean, Pireluve here wanted to apologize for the last prank we pulled on you."

"Alright." She took the box and opened it. When she saw what was in the box she screamed, dropped the box, and jumped backward. When she landed, she was at the edge of the dock. She lost her balance on the edge, and she fell. When she arose from the surface she was drowning.

"HELP ME!" She screamed, "I CAN'T SWIM!"

"OH MY GOD!" I yelled, "Pireluve, we've got to help her!"

He didn't hear me, he was too busy laughing his head off in the most sinister, and uncool way possible, so I dove into the water and dragged the girl towards the shore of the lake. She kept thrashing as I was holding onto her, which only made me have an even harder time trying to bring her to shore. I was only a kid too remember? I was eight years old, and I had to carry not only my weight to shore but also that of another child, who was also eight years old at the time, using only one of my arms to swim. It took me forever to carry her to the shore, but I finally did it. We were both breathing hard when we got to land. That's when Pireluve came around.

"What have you done?" he asked me, "You ruined the whole prank!"

"She was drowning," I protested in between my hard breaths, "We couldn't have let her drown, otherwise we would have killed her."

"She was never going to drown, but now, thanks to you, the prank is ruined. I would have thought that you would know the true meaning of mischief, but clearly, you don't. You fool!"

"If anyone is the fool, it's you Pireluve!" I yelled back at him.

"And with that, we are no longer friends!"

He scooped up some sand into his hand and he threw it at us. Some of the sand hit my eyes, and it burned my eyes. The girl was luckier than me; she only got sand in her long blonde hair. I covered my eyes with my hands thinking that it could stop the burning sense I was feeling.

"I hope you and your girlfriend are happy together!" he yelled as he ran away.

The girl scooped up some water to clean the sand out of my eyes. I removed my hands as the girl washed away the sand. My eyes would still burn even after all the sand had left my eyes. It took her a few scoops of water before all the sand was gone.

"Thanks," I said, rubbing my eyes so the burning sensation would dull.

"You're welcome, Dracollus."

"How do you know my name?" I asked skeptically because I never told the girl my name, nor any people who I pulled pranks on. I always gave Pireluve's name whenever we did pranks together.

"Everybody knows who the 'Duo Pranksters' are: Dracollus and Pireluve. The real question is, do you know who I am?"

"No," I admitted sheepishly.

"Well, I am Jamano, and thank you for saving my life."

"Well, I kind of put it in trouble in the first place."

"But at least you were able to correct your mistake."

"Jamano?" a voice said out of nowhere. "Ancient Gods, what happened to you?"

Over by the docks was a boy. He had short brown hair and was very tall for a kid his age. At the time, he was nine years old and he was 3'9. He came over running towards Jamano.

"Are you OK?" he asked her.

"I'm fine, Haruasore, thanks to Dracollus here."

"Hey!" He said when he saw me, "Aren't you that guy that keeps pulling pranks on people with that other guy? I never found any of those pranks to be funny."

"I used to do pranks," I admitted, "but I no longer do. That other guy is not my friend, at least, not anymore."

"What made you stop?"

"I stopped when I jeopardized Jamano's life here. I guess it was a calling that it was time for me to stop."

"Well, if you saved Jamano's life, and you are no longer a friend of Pireluve, then I guess you can be my friend."

"Thanks, Haruasore was it?" I asked.

"That's right Dracollus." Haruasore said, "We are going to be the best of friends!"

Chapter 13

An Old Friend is the New Enemy

Now let's go back to the story. Pireluve came out of the wood with a mean look in his gray eyes and a sword in its sheath by his side. Sylfano demanded, "What are you doing here, Pireluve?"

"I could ask the exact same thing of you, Sylfano," he said, "Considering you should be dead."

Sylfano looked offended. "Excuse me?"

Pireluve looked at me. "You were supposed to kill her, Dracollus. It was what you were destined to do."

"What are you talking about Pireluve?" I asked, confused. "I would never hurt anyone, much less kill someone. Oh, and another thing, you don't know anything about me or my destiny at all."

"You know, you're right. I know nothing about you anymore, but when we used to work together when we were little kids, I thought I saw the true you. The PART OF YOU that was evil; the part of you that was on my side of the war and not on her side." He then pointed to Sylfano.

"My side," she asked. "What do you mean by 'on my side of the war'?"

"I'm really surprised that your dragon senses can't detect what I am. Then again, you can only sense danger, and right now I am the biggest threat you have ever seen."

"How do you know that I am a dragon and how do you know so much about dragons?"

"That is something…"

"Your Highness!" A voice called out for Sylfano.

We all turned around to find Jacob, Haruasore and Jamano. Jacob was holding a sword with a blue blade in his hand and Haruasore was holding a piece of paper in his left hand while holding a knife with a blue blade in his right hand. Jamano, on the other hand, held nothing but stood behind her boyfriend and his mentor.

"Sylfano," Jacob said, "Stay away from that boy over there, he's dangerous."

"Dracollus," Haruasore said, "you need to stay behind us. We will protect you from him."

"What is there to protect us from?" I asked him. "I could take down this old friend of mine in one blow."

"You could," Haruasore said, "but he is not alone in this world."

"So, you know what I am, Haruasore?" Pireluve asked Haruasore.

"We only found out when we searched your transport and found this letter." He then put the paper out in front of him to show Pireluve. Using my enhanced vision, I could see the wording on the paper. The wording was in another language that I didn't know what it was. Surprisingly, I could read what was on the piece of paper. One line said, '*Find the princess and whoever is with her.*' Then Haruasore said. "Even though none of us can read what this says, we still have a good idea of WHAT you are, and that would mean that you are not a regular Helmam now, are you?"

"Of course I am not!" he said with a crooked smile. "I knew what I was at the age of four. That's why I wanted to make this place miserable because that is what I am supposed to do. My mission was to pave the way for chaos to come to this place. I brought along Dracollus with me to make Housay a worse place to live, but he tricked me into thinking he was one of us, and it turns out that he is one of them."

"One of what?" I asked. "None of you are not making any sense."

"Oh, come on." Jamano said, "Do we really have to spell it out for you, Dracollus?"

"Uh no, you don't," I said sarcastically. "I already know what he is."

"Well, it is better to I show you what I am instead of explaining what I am," Pireluve exclaimed.

"NO!" Everyone else besides me yelled.

"TOO LATE!" Pireluve sneered.

He curled his fingers and flexed his arms, and he brought down his arms to his side and a gust of wind came from the ground underneath him, making his black hair go straight up. That's when the ground started to open. Standing straight was a little difficult to do as the ground was moving. The shaking ground was not like a landquake, but like someone was opening/moving the ground underneath us. A dozen sets of hands emerged from the cracks on the ground. Very slowly, hands became arms, until they showed us the bodies and faces of eleven Gargoyles. There was another head, but this one was made of stone, and it had glowing red eyes on it.

"Pireluve," I said, "Who…what are you?!"

"He's a stone lord!" Haruasore bellowed. "He can summon gargoyles, it's what they do!"

"OH NOW, YOU TELL ME!"

"This is the end for you dragons and for your friends," Pireluve announced.

"Let the invasion of the Housay begin NOW!"

Chapter 14

The Invasion Begins

I thrust my hand forward and shot a column of fire towards a gargoyle, turning it into a pile of ashes before it fully emerged from the ground. The rest of the gargoyles came out of the ground and flew into the air. Now that they were out of the ground, I could see what they looked like. Their faces and ears were like bats, while their bodies were human but very muscular. Their legs were long with talons as toes. Every part of them was gray except for their faces, which were brown. They were all delta gargoyles. I wonder if I burned the omega gargoyle for a split second. Then the gargoyles started to form a three by two formation. That is when the head came out of stone in full form. The entire body, arms, hand, and legs were made for stone. This thing was a golem.

"Is it normal for a stone lord to summon a golem?" I asked Sylfano.

"No." She replied, "Not unless he is a member of the Ancient Stone Lords. And in this case, he is. LOOK OUT!"

The golem hurled a giant rock from the crack in the ground and threw it at me. I jumped to the left to dodge the rock. That is when the gargoyles started their attack. The first two opened their mouth and out came a green rotating crescent. I don't know how I could see the green crescent, but I didn't like them. The rotating crescents were aimed at Sylfano, Jacob and Haruasore. They were able to dodge them with some element of luck due to the high velocity of the crescents. The crescents kept advancing to their previous location, and when they hit the ground, they exploded into red-orange fireballs.

"Was that their crushing wave?" I asked as I dodged another rock thrown from the golem.

"No, it is not!" she yelled as she dodged another wave of crescents. "That's their wave of discord."

The gargoyles in the front row retreated to the back. The next row of gargoyles advanced. Before they could do anything, I used my ice powers to freeze one of the gargoyles. Once again I thrust my hand, out but this time, I concentrated to freeze the air around the gargoyle. The gargoyle became frozen instantaneously, turning pale as it plummeted to the ground, and shattered into a thousand fragments.

"Great job, Dracollus!" I heard Jamano cheer.

I turned around to see that she was hiding behind a tree like a little girl. I mean who could blame her? She had no way to defend herself.

"LOOK OUT!" Jacob warned, "This is their crushing wave attack."

I looked at the front to see the gargoyles. The remaining gargoyles broke out of formation and flew side by side. They looked like they were going to be sick. When they opened their mouths, they released a glowing purple line that grew as they left the mouths of the gargoyles. The purple lines approached Sylfano and Jacob slowly. They dodged them with ease but the lines just ripped a line in the ground where they had been standing.

"That is what the crushing lines do," Sylfano explained. "They cut anything in their path. Now it's time to really heat the place up."

She transformed herself into a dragon. Jacob got on her back and they flew into the smoke-filled sky. I dropped to one knee, put my hands on the ground and closed my eyes in concentration. As the exploding feeling developed inside me, claws sprouted out from my nails, wings sprouted out from my shoulder blades, my nose became a snout, and my body, legs, and arms became all scaly. My transformation took a few seconds to be complete. When I was done, I beckoned to Haruasore, "Hop on my back!"

"No, thanks," he replied, "I'll take on Pireluve. You and Sylfano can take care of the gargoyles."

He advanced to attack Pireluve. I took flight and caught up with Sylfano. She was trying to break up the formation of the gargoyles with fireballs that she was hurling from her mouth. The gargoyles would always dodge them, but they would always go back into their formation from whatever direction they dodged. Then the unthinkable cool thing happened. When the gargoyles tried to regroup for a second time, Jacob Mas Pal jumped off the back of Sylfano and got on the back of a gargoyle. The gargoyle fell to the ground and Jacob plunged his sword to the gargoyles back. The gargoyle screamed and as it disintegrated into a pile of ashes.

"Is that what happens to gargoyles when they die?" I asked Jacob as he regained his balance.

"Only if they are killed with a blade made of sapphire." He replied. "Not only does sapphire hurt gargoyles, but it also burns them. Now please land so I can take out more gargoyles."

I landed on the ground and allowed Jacob to sit on my back. We then flew into the sky. I shot a couple of icicles towards some of the gargoyles, but they dodged them. That is when Sylfano came from behind and shot a column of fire towards three of them and roasted them to a pile of ashes.

"GREAT SHOT!" I said to her transpathically.

"Thanks," she replied transpathically, "but this battle is not over yet."

I was so hung on the fact that Sylfano took out a bunch of gargoyles that I didn't notice that a boulder was coming towards me.

"WATCH OUT!" Jacob hollered to me.

The warning was too late. The boulder struck me on my face, sending me to a spiral down to the ground. Jacob was able to jump off my back and land softly on his feet, while I landed hard. I was dazed but somehow, I could still hear the battles.

"NO!" Sylfano yelled.

In response, she shot a column of fire towards the golem. The golem just stood there for a second and then the golem collapsed into a pile of pebbles. Sylfano flew low to check on me, but before she got a chance a gargoyle hurled a wave of discord towards her and she was hit on her side. She sustained a giant cut. She smashed next to me, and then she changed back to her Helmam form.

"Brave effort you did there, your Highness," Pireluve said from behind me.

"What did you do to Haruasore?" I bellowed, unable to look at his face because I was too weak to turn my head around.

"Your friend is just fine. He is just unconscious for now. It turns out that I am a bit stronger and more skilled than he is. Now as for you Jacob - any last words to your princess?"

"YOU WILL NOT KILL HER!" he said. "You'll have to get past me first!"

"Very well then. I guess I have to take out both of you after all."

At that point, I lost consciousness, and transformed back to my Helmam form.

■ ■

As I slowly regained consciousness, there was absolute destruction everywhere. There were trees destroyed (including the oldest tree in the center of the Iris), scorch marks on the ground right next to Sylfano as if some of the gargoyles had tried using their wave of discord around her. Jacob and Pireluve continued fighting. Jacob was missing his left hand but he remained fearless. Pireluve had his sword drawn out and wielded a black shield. The shield was exactly like the one I had seen in my dream, which meant that I was going to protect Sylfano soon. I couldn't see any of the gargoyles that Pireluve had summoned. Either they had all left, or they were all killed. Or maybe they were out of time to spend here. I remembered how Jacob told me that summoned gargoyles only have a certain amount of time to roam this planet. Maybe it was past their limit to remain here. Then again, I had no idea how long I had been out. Jacob swung his sword at Pireluve's shield. Pireluve thrust forward his arm that held his shield and Jacob lost his grip on his sword. The sword flew through the air and landed a good five krompus away from Jacob. Pireluve brought his sword back and plunged it into Jacob's heart.

"Looks like you have failed your princess," Pireluve said to Jacob.

"At least I protected her with my last breath." he retorted with great effort. "And got rid of the last of your gargoyles that were still able to roam this land before they were reduced to a pile of dirt. I have fulfilled my role as Sylfano's Dragon-lord."

"But you still failed."

Pireluve pulled out his sword from Jacob, who fell to the ground, dead. I tried to move only to find out that I couldn't. It was only then that I realized that this was all a dream. I tried to wake myself up but I couldn't.

"YOU'LL PAY FOR KILLING JACOB!" A voice yelled behind me. I tried to move my head to see where the voice came from but I could not. Pireluve turned to where the voice came from.

"And how exactly am I going to pay by the likes of you, Jamano?" Pireluve mocked her. "Because if memory serves correctly, you were hiding behind a tree. Which means that you were either too scared to fight or you have no skills in fighting, and in this case you are both."

"I may not have skills," she reasoned. "But he does!" She pointed right behind him where Haruasore had picked up Jacob's sword. Pireluve turned around to see that Haruasore was making his stand.

"So you think you can take on me now with that sword?" Pireluve asked Haruasore.

"I most definitely can now," he said with great confidence. "The last time you caught me off guard. I am not letting my guard down again."

"We shall just see about that!"

The two then went onwards for another round of skirmish. Haruasore demonstrated that he was very skilled with a sword. I knew that he was not formally trained in self-defense, but I had no idea that meant he was also an expert with a sword in his hands. The way he could use the handle of the blade in one hand was amazing. If he needed to exert more force in his strikes he would use both of his hands on the handle then swing. What's more surprising to me was that Haruasore could switch hands that he held the sword in. At the very beginning of this round, Haruasore was using his left hand. Whenever I saw him in class I knew, he would only use his right hand to write, pick things up, or catch things. At the beginning of the duel, I was wondering why he was using his left hand. When he needed to use a more powerful strike, he gripped the handle with both hands and made his strike. After he was done, he was holding his sword with his right hand. It was only that occurred to me Haruasore could use both his hands to do whatever he needed his hands to do. Haruasore was trying to confuse Pireluve! The duel took what seemed like an hour, with no one looking like they were gaining the upper hand before things started to change for the worst.

"You seem to be better with handling a sword than a knife," Pireluve remarked, not taking a moment to stop.

"I should," Haruasore said as he locked his sword with Pireluve's. "I am a descendant of one of the few survivors of the battle of the Divided. There is nothing that I WOULD NOT do to regain the family honor."

"Well then, I'm sure this next move of mine will not surprise you then."

Pireluve had broken away from Haruasore's and his crossed swords. He then used his shield to knock Haruasore to the ground by hitting him in the face. Haruasore hit the ground pretty hard. That's when we all heard a noise behind us. I couldn't see what it was, but it sounded like someone was grunting. Pireluve looked at me, (to be more precise he was looking behind me.) That's when he noticed Sylfano starting to move.

"I guess now is my only chance to kill her while she is at her weakest," he said out loud.

That's when I actually woke up. I lifted myself off the ground to see that Sylfano was struggling to stand up, and Pireluve was charging right at Sylfano!

"PIRELUVE NOOOOOOOO!!" I yelled and jumped in front of Sylfano.

Haruasore was starting to get off the ground when he noticed what was about to happen. Pireluve brought his sword back and then lunged it forward. I felt an intense, excruciating pain in my chest! I looked down. His sword was plunged into my chest.

Chapter 15

Darkness and Pain

Everybody but Pireluve was yelling in distress. Haruasore charged forward and brought the sword back behind his head. He swung the sword forward right at Pireluve's neck. The blade passed through his neck instantly, blood splattered all over my face, and Pireluve's head rolled to the ground. The body of Pireluve tumbled to the ground. I couldn't feel anything for a split second and then I fell backward, but Sylfano caught me.

"Dracollus!" She said with a worried look on her face as I looked up to it. "Stay calm, you're going to be alright."

Jamano and Haruasore ran to my side, both on opposite sides of me. It was then that Haruasore took the sword in my chest out. I groaned in pain as the blade exited my chest. I was breathing heavily now. It was very painful to breathe. It was if someone was crushing my insides every time I took a breath.

"Dracollus," Jamano said trying really hard not to cry, "Look at me and relax. Everything will be alright once you start to heal."

"He's not going to heal," Haruasore said while he examined the blade of the sword.

"What are you talking about, Haruasore? Of course, he's going to heal. It's one of his powers, remember?"

"Yes, I remember, but the blade he was struck with is made of obsidian. Which means that the wound will not heal until he is dead. That is what obsidian does to dragons if they are injured by it. The only known way to cure something a wound like this is with magic, and none of us know how to cure it."

"Don't worry about me," I said with a shaky breath. "Leave me here to die."

"Absolutely not!" Haruasore screamed, "We are not going to let you die here alone. We… We will be here with you until … until..."

"Then leave my body here then. You guys have to… have to get to my parents and… and tell them what… happened and what is going to happen."

"What is going to happen?" Sylfano asked me.

"Pireluve said…" Dark spots had started begin to show in my vision, "he said that the invasion of Housay had… had begun. Tell them not to worry about me yet. Tell them… that they have to protect their home from the gargoyles. Tell them… That I have loved … always loved them." The pain in my chest had grown into an unbearable pain now. The pain had spread towards the lower half of my body, and I knew that I would only have a few more seconds to live.

"Dracollus," Sylfano said, tears now cascading down her lovely cheeks. "I really wish we had more time together."

"I… I… do… do… too." Darkness then took complete control over my vision.

Time seemed to cascade down, as I lay dead. At first, I could not feel anything. I don't know how much time passed before I actually realized that I could now feel pain. Nothing but pain; that was all I could think about now. I knew that I was dead, but you would think that the pain would be over now. Instead, the pain was so strong that if my heart were still beating it would probably be beating as fast as a helicopter blade. That's when it dawned on me that my heart was beating again!

Then I saw a golden light in front of me. It was very pretty. The light seemed to be moving closer and closer to me. When it completely filled my vision, I realized that the pain had been replaced with a feeling of warmth. Welcoming warmth, which became warmer, then hotter until it felt like I was on fire with flames consuming my limbs.

That's when I opened my eyes again and gasped for air. For a split second, I thought I was in heaven or in paradise. Then I realized I was exactly where I died, minus my friends. They must have left me like I asked them to do. I removed my Shirt to check my chest to see if my wound was still there. The wound was no longer there, but on my shoulder, there was a mark. It looked like a B, an E and an R were formed together, with the end of the R Looped. It looked something like this:

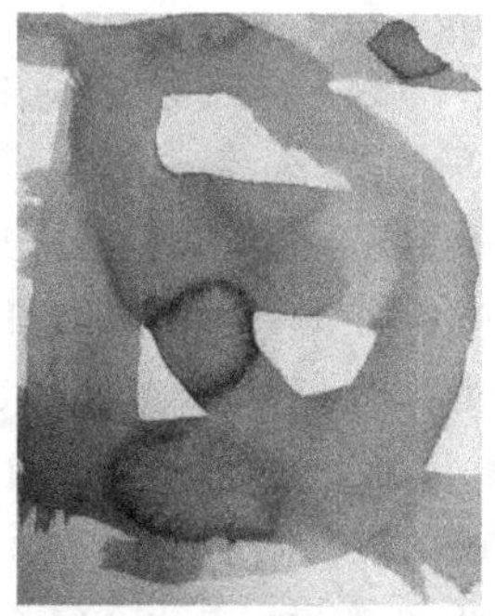

I don't know how I was alive again, but I was pretty sure that this mark was the answer. I put my shirt back on, and I sensed trouble in the industrial district. I don't know how in the world I knew there was danger at the time, but later on, I would know the answer to a lot of things.

I'm getting sidetracked. Going back to the story, when I sensed that some kind of danger I transformed into my dragon form and flew to the industrial district, not knowing where my instincts would take me. I flew much faster than I normally would and got to my destination within seconds rather than minutes. When I got to my destination I saw the same scene I saw in my dreams. Sylfano was on the road with her leg stuck in a pile of rubble, and the building was about to collapse on her. Time seemed to have slowed down because the building that was falling all of a sudden slowed down. I dove towards her and moved the rubble away with my paw, and got her in my other paw and flew to the other end of the street. Just in time, too, for the building had collapsed on the street completely with just a few seconds for us to spare. I put Sylfano down on the ground. I transformed into my Helmam form and said,

"Are you alright?"

Sylfano was speechless.

"D-D-Dracollus?" she blurted.

"Yeah, it's me, alive somehow."

She put her hand on my shoulder and then gave me a very tight hug.

"WHOA! Easy with the crushing-me-to-death squeeze." I said. "I only just got back from the dead a few seconds ago."

She broke up our hug then.

"How in the name of the universe are you ALIVE?"

"I don't have the slightest clue, but I bet it has something with the mark on my shoulder."

"What mark?"

There was a screeching sound in the air right behind me.

"I'll tell you more about it later. Right now we have much bigger problems."

I turned around to see a flock of six gargoyles flying above the ruins of the building that had just collapsed.

"Curses!" The Omega said, "There is another dragon here, I thought that there was only one dragon. That being the princess of the Ancient Dragons here!" The omega looked very similar to the deltas but, he had his wings on his shoulder blades, and he had claws instead of fingers.

"Who cares about the other dragon?" a Delta said to the Omega. "Let's just kill them both!"

The Delta opened its mouth and shot a crushing wave at me. Instead of dodging the attack, I held my ground and crossed my arms in front of me.

"DRACOLLUS LOOK OUT!" Sylfano yelled.

But I didn't move. Some part of me wanted to stand my ground for some reason. When the crushing wave reached my arms it did not cut them, instead, the crushing wave stayed where it was on my arm. When I pushed my arms forward and uncrossed my arms, the crushing wave careened toward the Delta gargoyle that shot it at me with such great speed that the gargoyle did not have time to dodge it. The crushing wave passed through the gargoyle's body instantly, and both halves of the gargoyle fell to the ground.

"How did you do that?" the Omega shrieked.

I didn't know how I did what I did so I said, "I'm a dragon that is full of surprises. Here is another one."

I put my hand out then I shaped my hand into an O. I then brought my hand behind my head. As I brought my hand behind my head, I used my ice ability to freeze the air that was inside my hand to make a spear made out of ice. I then threw the spear at the Omega aiming for its heart, but one of the deltas went in front of the omega and took the icicle spear instead. The spear penetrated the chest of the gargoyle, and it fell to the ground dead.

"An Ice dragon!" one of the last two deltas said. "That is something the spy should have told us."

"I'm afraid your little spy is dead," I said. "My friend silenced him permanently. He won't be giving you any more information about my friends or me."

All the gargoyles were surprised by this news.

"SCREAM SQUAD RETREAT!" the Omega said as he fled the scene. The rest of the gargoyles followed him. Once they were out of view, I turned to Sylfano and said,

"Where is Haruasore anyway?"

Sylfano was speechless again.

"You just…a crushing wave. You just…"

"Yeah, I know I blocked it, but can we worry about that later? I need to see Haruasore."

"Dracollus?" A voice came from behind me.

I turned toward the voice to see Jamano and Haruasore standing next to each other. Haruasore had a cut on his arm, and his face was covered in soot. Other than that he looked OK. Jamano looked fine, except for the 'Am I Dreaming' look on her face

"GUYS!" I ran towards them and hugged them.

"Wow!" said Haruasore, "You're…alive?"

I broke away from them.

"Yeah, I know! Isn't it great that I'm alive again?!"

"But how?" Jamano asked.

"I wish I knew!"

"I bet I do." Sylfano offered.

I turned around and asked her, "You do?"

"First show us that mark on your shoulder that you were talking about earlier."

"What mark?" Haruasore and Jamano said in unison.

I rolled up my Shirt sleeve and showed everyone my mark. Haruasore gasped and dropped the sword that he was holding in his hand.

"I knew it!" Sylfano said.

"What?" I asked her. "You knew what? What does this mark mean?"

"It's impossible," Haruasore said, "but now it all makes sense."

"Can someone please tell me what this mark means, please?"

Sylfano looked at me with a serious look. "That mark that is on your shoulder," she declared, "means that you are the Bringer of the Dragons."

Chapter 16

The Bringer

I could have said a thousand things after being told this. I could have said something like "Yeah I knew that." and "Are you kidding me?" or maybe even "All this time I was the Bringer of the Dragons?", but instead, I said,

"But why did this mark only appear after I died?"

"I don't know, Dracollus," Sylfano replied. "But one thing is clear to all of us, you are destined to save us all."

"WHOA.WHOA. WHOA." Jamano said sticking her hands out to calm all of us down a bit. "Wait a minute, can someone please explain to me what the Helmamnor the Bringer of the Dragons is?"

Haruasore covered his mouth with his hand as he giggled at this. "I keep forgetting that you are not in the loop about these things. Anyhow, the Bringer of the Dragons is supposed to unite the gargoyles and the dragons in peace with the Bringer of the Gargoyles. These two Bringers are supposed to end the war. It is Dracollus' destiny to end the war with the Bringer of the Gargoyles."

"But who is the Bringer of the Gargoyles?" Jamano asked.

"We don't know yet. The Bringer of Gargoyles is supposed to be revealed after the Bringer of the Dragons - that's what the prophecy says."

"But what is the prophecy?" Jamano and I asked in unison.

Jamano looked at me confused. "How do you not know the prophecy?" She asked me.

"I only found out the night I fell asleep for 41 hours. Which reminds me," I turned towards Sylfano, "how long have I been dead for?"

"Oh uh," she said, hesitantly, "You were dead for… what time is it now?"

"It is 17 minutes past 1 pm. In other words; 1:17." I shook my head after I said that. "How did I know that?"

"It's one of your new powers," Sylfano said. "Not only can you know what time it is, but you can slow down time a little."

"That's cool."

"Now to answer your question you were dead for a good twelve hours. You died at 6:15, since it's been about two minutes since you were revived I'd say."

Just then there was an explosion from the west.

"What was that?" I asked.

"***OH BLISH!!!***" Sylfano said as she put her hands to her head. "We forgot about the other gargoyles that were here in Housay. We have to hurry. They could go after your guardians, Dracollus."

"*Ilsa and Lunfa*!" I yelled, "Come on, guys! Hop on my back!"

I concentrated to transform myself to my dragon form. Again, there was this feeling like my insides were about to explode, prior to my transformation. Jamano and Haruasore hopped on my back as Sylfano transformed into her dragon. Sylfano and I flew into the sky with great speed, as Jamano screamed.

"What the matter?" I asked her transpathically as I flew.

"I have never ridden on a dragon before!" she screamed.

"Neither have I!" Haruasore yelled so he can be heard against the roaring wind in my ears. "This speed is awesome, and the ride is so comfortable. I wish we could do travel like this every time we needed to go somewhere!"

We made it to the Middle District within a matter of seconds. I looked to see where the explosion came from. It turned out that the explosion came from a block away from the high school. Which means that it was only two blocks away from my home.

"*Mom, dad*!" I yelled.

I flew into the direction of my house to see what caused the explosion. When I got to the scene of the explosion, there was a man lying down on his stomach on the ground, next to a big crater that was about 20 krompus long in diameter. I dove to the ground and landed on my paws.

"Check to see who that man is," I said to Haruasore.

Haruasore got off my back and turned the man over. We all gasped because the man on the ground was Lunfa. There was a slash wound on his right side, and it looked as if something bit him on the neck. His eyes were closed, so I could not tell if he was dead or just unconscious. Haruasore checked for a pulse on his wrist.

"I'm very sorry, Dracollus," he said with a very sad look in his eyes, "he's dead."

"And that is what is going to happen to all of you!" A creepy and very low voice emerged from behind me. I turned my head and long neck to the direction where the voice came from. The voice belonged to an Omega gargoyle that was flying in the air with his flock of seven deltas.

"What have you done to Ilsa?" I said to them. "Tell me or you will suffer my wrath."

"OH I'M SACRED!" the Omega said to me sarcastically. "But if you want to know, you'll have to learn the hard way." With that, he sent out a crushing wave towards me. I deflected it, with a swing from my tail, sending it in the direction of a delta. The crushing wave passed through the delta easily, and the delta fell to the ground. All the gargoyles were so surprised by this.

"How did you do that?" the Omega asked me.

"Tell me what you did to my mother now!" I yelled. "Or how I deflected your crushing wave will be the least of your worries."

"Uh, well your mother-"

He was cut off because a lightning bolt hit his wing. The lightning bolt passed through his wing making a hole in it. The gargoyle screamed as he fell to the ground.

"*Leave my son alone*!" a voice came from the left.

I turned my head and saw that my mother was standing there. Her face was covered in sweat, her hair was a rat's nest, and her clothes had wrinkles on them.

"*Mom*!" I yelled. "You're alright."

"Just a little tired but I'll be ok."

I then turned my focus on the gargoyles. "Now I'm going to let you live this time, because I'm a fair Helmam and dragon, but if any more gargoyles attack Housay, then I will kill you all of you!"

"*Who are you*?" The gargoyles insisted.

"I am the Bringer of the Dragons," I said with great confidence, "and I will end this war." I then blew a column of fire towards the gargoyles as they fled, carrying their Omega with them.

I transformed back into a Helmam when the gargoyles left. I ran to my mother and hugged her.

"I thought I'd never see you again!" I said.

"Well, we could have been in a better position if you did not lie to the gargoyles." my mother said.

"I did not lie! I told them the truth! Look! Look!"

I showed her the mark on my shoulder and she gasped. "So it is true, you ARE the Bringer of the Dragons."

"Yes, it is and we only found this out after I died."

"Wait… You what after you WHAT?"

I looked at my friends, "You guys never told her?"

"No, we did not," Sylfano said. "By the time we got to the Industrial District, the place was under attack by gargoyles."

"Before we could even tell your mother that you had died," Haruasore said, "the highway exploded. That is when the gargoyles started to attack us."

"OK then. Mom, here's what happened in the forest district." I told her the story of how I died. When I was finished with my story she didn't say anything at first, but then she said, "You died?"

"Yeah, and now I am back from the dead," I said.

"And now you've come to end the war."

"Yes, that is true," I said. "But right now we have to liberate the remaining gargoyles here in Housay. We better get to work." I looked at Sylfano. "How do you want to do this?"

"Why are you asking me?" Sylfano asked.

"Well, you ARE the Princess of the Ancient Dragons, so technically you are supposed to lead us!"

"Yes, but you are the Bringer of the Dragons, and you are supposed to end the war!"

"Good point." I thought of a plan to divide us so we can eliminate any gargoyles. "Alright here's what's going to happen Sylfano, I want you and Haruasore to check the Rich, Industrial, Ancient, and Forest Districts. I know we just came from the Forest and Industrial District, but I want to be safe and make sure there aren't any more gargoyles there. My mother and I will check what is left of the Middle District, the Working District, and the Farming District. Let's all meet up at my house when all this is over."

"What about me?" Jamano asked, "What is going to happen to me?"

"I want you to run to my house and lock the doors and windows." I said, "My mother put a spell over the house to protect it from gargoyles."

"Ok. Thank you." She ran in the direction of my house.

"The spell you put on the house protects the house from gargoyles, right?" I asked my mother.

"Originally the spell I cast over the house was meant to keep gargoyles from entering the house." She said. "But when the invasion happened, your father and I put a shielding spell over the house. And yes, the shielding spell protects the house from gargoyle attacks.”

"Ok great! Now let's go, guys, we have tons of stuff to do!”

■■

It was a little odd for my mother to be riding on my back now that I'm a teenager. I used to ride on her back when I was a kid, but now it is her turn. I was thinking about this as we flew towards the farming district. There were no signs of gargoyles in the Middle District, so my mother and I decided to check the Farming District. When we arrived at the Farming District there were lots of dead bodies on the ground. This is the most vulnerable district of all the districts. Most of the bodies had gashes on their sides. Some were cut in half, while others had bite marks. What these gargoyles do to these Helmams is barbaric. I kept flying into the Farming District until I came across this one body of a little girl. I did not know the girl at first, but her Shirt looked extremely familiar. I landed on the ground and turned the body over with my paw. The girl had half her side missing, but what freaked me out the most was the girl's face. I knew this little girl: this was Jamano's little sister.

"Oh, no.” I wailed, "This will break Jamano's heart! What was she even doing here?”

"If my memory serves me correctly, her mother told me that they were going to this District to get some things."

"What sort of things?"

"I don't remember. While I was still on the portacall with Jamano's mother, the Middle District was under attack by the gargoyles."

"And that is what happened here." A high-pitched voice said from overhead.

I looked up and saw a flock of sixteen gargoyles overhead. Their omega was huge and had wings that were about three krompus long. This omega looked different from the other omegas I had seen earlier. Instead of his entire body being gray, it was black, and his face was gray.

"You shall join your little friend in death," the Omega said.

"I have already known what that feels like, so why don't you give it a try?"

I shot an icicle towards the Omega from my mouth, and it penetrated his chest instantly. He just laughed and removed the icicle out from his chest. The wound healed in a matter of seconds.

"Nice try, Ice Dragon," he said, "But I am an Ancient Gargoyle, and I can only be killed by-" He stopped talking and clutched his chest. Just then the wound in his chest grew back and the wound spread throughout his chest and body.

"HOW did you do that?" he gasped.

"I probably should have told you that I am the Bringer of the Dragons," I said. "So I can vanquish anyone!"

"NOOOO!" The gargoyle broke into a thousand pieces and fell to the ground. The remaining gargoyles started shaking.

"I will let you guys go," I vowed. "But if you guys ever attack Housay again, I will hunt you all down and kill each and every one of you."

"Thank you for your kindness," one of the deltas said. Then they all scampered away.

When they were gone, my mother said to me, "You should not have let them leave."

"I am the Bringer of the Dragons." I snapped. "If I don't show some mercy to gargoyles, then what is the point of bringing an end to the war?"

My mother thought about it for a while. "Alright," she finally said, "I guess you're right."

"Now that that's all settled, let's go to the Working District."

We arrived at the Working District only to find it standing in one piece. Not a single item was damaged. This district did not seem to have been attacked. We headed back to the Middle District. I was in no hurry to tell Jamano the terrible news.

When we got to the house, Sylfano and Haruasore were waiting for us.

"How did everything go?" Haruasore asked me. "We only had to clear out gargoyles in the Rich

District and the Ancient District, the other two districts were in the clear. Then again, we weren't sure if any gargoyles had attacked the Ancient District, considering all the damage that you had done to the Forbidden Area. I mean really, out of both areas to attack they had to attack the district that was already literally half destroyed. Does that make any sense to anyone?"

"No," I said. "As for me and my mother, we only encountered gargoyles in the Farming District."

"What's wrong?" Sylfano asked me. "You look terrible."

"Where's Jamano?"

Sylfano looked confused. "She's still in the house. Why?"

"I have something to tell her - something very tragic."

"What is it?" Haruasore asked me.

"I think it'll better if we were all together when I tell Jamano."

We entered the house. Jamano was in the living room, sitting on the couch.

"Oh, thank the Ancient Gods!" she hollered as she ran to us. She hugged Haruasore first and then me.

"I thought you guys were dead. No offense, Dracollus."

"None taken," I said sadly.

"Dracollus, what's wrong?"

"Jamano, I'm… I'm very, very…sorry to tell you this but-" I stopped, unable to continue.

"When we were at the Farming District," my mother said. "We found your little sister's …body."

Jamano was petrified and had a horrified look on her face.

"NO! You're lying!" She yelled. "My sister is alright! She's alive and probably reading a book about magic!"

I hugged her. She tried to push me away, and then she started to cry. She cried for a full thirty minutes.

"Everything else will be alright, honey," Haruasore said to her after she calmed down. "We've all lost someone we care about. For Sylfano and me, it was Jacob Mas Pal. Dracollus lost his father. But now that he is the Bringer of the Dragons, we will lose no one else."

"Haruasore," I blurted, "knock it off!"

"No, he's right," Sylfano said. "Thanks to you there will be no more collateral damages from the war."

"I don't even know what to do." I protested.

"You'll know what to do when the time is right. Speaking of which, it is now the right time for you to know the prophecy."

Sylfano sat down on a couch. She took a deep breath, looked at me and then she recited the prophecy:

"One child of the dragons
And one child of the gargoyles
Shall bring the two sides together
And bring peace between the races
The Dragon shall appear first
With the Gargoyle completing the peace
Two lovers shall be united
And war as we know it
Shall be brought to an end."

"That's the prophecy," Sylfano concluded.

"What about the rest?" I asked.

"What do you mean?"

"Well, it sounds like there should be more of the prophecy."

"Well, if there was more, the old Dragon prophet never mentioned it. Speaking of which, we have to find the prophet of the Dragons."

"Why?" Jamano asked.

"If we find the prophet, he might know where to find the Bringer of the Gargoyles, and the sooner we find the Bringer of the Gargoyles, the sooner this war can end!"

Chapter 17

The Truth about My Journey

Everybody left to go to his or her house soon afterward. We agreed to meet up at Sylfano's house after we finished packing. Jamano wanted to come because she wanted to be with Haruasore. I did not believe her at first, but Sylfano said that maybe we should let her come along. She had a feeling that she would be very useful later. I wondered how Jamano was going to be useful, but I also did not want to leave behind Jamano while the rest of us were off on this mission. I went to my room and started packing some things in a travel bag: Shirts, pants to hide my golden scaly legs, sweaters, a water bottle to help master my water bending, and the necklace that I received for my birthday. This was the last gift that my father gave me while he was still alive, and it was the only thing that I had left of him.

My mother came into my room. "Have you finished packing?" she asked.

"Yup," I said cheerfully. "I'm all ready for my trip to the Ancient Kingdom of the Dragons."

Sylfano said that we had to go to the Ancient Kingdom of the Dragons first. The only person who knew where to look for the dragon prophet was her father, the King of the Ancient Dragons. She also said that she wanted to see her father after being away from him for so long.

"Right. Well, before you go…" my mother confided, "I have something for you."

She took a tiny box out of her pocket and handed it to me.

"What is it?" I asked.

"Open it and see."

I opened the box and inside there was a silver ring. I took the ring out of the box. It was a spinning ring and the band that was spinney had an interesting design on it. It looked like it was a maze, but it was not. It looked like a labyrinth or a symbol for balance.

"Cool. But why are you giving this to me?"

"That ring belonged to your father. He made it for you, and he wanted you to have it."

I was confused for a second; Lunfa was terrible at making pottery. He couldn't even make a pot, much less a ring.

"I never knew that dad could make rings."

"That's because it is not Lunfa's ring. That ring was made by your birth father."

I was stunned and speechless for a few seconds. Finally, I said, "Why didn't you give this to me earlier?"

"Your father instructed me to give it to you when I thought you needed it the most because that is no ordinary ring that you are holding - that is a dragon ring. Each ring is meant to do something to the dragon that wears it. Put it on, and let us see what it can do."

I put the ring on my middle finger. The second it settled on my finger, I felt immensely stronger.

"WOW!" I said with so much enthusiasm.

"What happened?" my mother asked me.

"I feel stronger. This ring gives more power!"

"I'm glad that it strengthens you because I have something to confess to you." My mother then took a deep breath. "Has Sylfano told you the name of the Dragon Prophet?"

I was confused by this question. I said, "No. What does this have to do with anything?"

"The Dragon Prophet's name is Allidan, and he…" my mother paused to collect her thoughts. "…he is your birth father."

I was speechless again. "You … knew the identity of my father all this time?" I asked, a bit upset.

"I'm sorry, Dracollus that I did not tell you earlier. I was trying to protect you. When I found out that you could dream of the future, I realized who your father was, and if Sylfano found out that you were his son she would have never helped you."

"Why is that?"

"Your father was banished for a reason. I don't know why specifically, but if Sylfano found out about you, she could have used you to get to your father."

"I had a right to know! But you are right."

"Wait. You're forgiving me - just like that?" my mother asked, totally surprised.

"After all that I have been through, I think I should know by now to trust what you keep from me. I have to learn to know what is important for me to know and what should be kept secret."

"That's good, Dracollus," she said with a smile. "Now go kick some gargoyle wings, my son!"

"I will, Ilsa. Are you sure that you still want to stay here?" I asked.

"I do want to come with you, but Housay is my home and I do not want to leave this place vulnerable to more gargoyle attacks. I need to protect it while you save this world."

"I love you, Ilsa." I hugged her.

"I love you, too," she replied, now tearing up.

I took my bag, went outside my house and transformed into a dragon. I carried my bag with my paw and went to Sylfano's house. Sylfano was waiting for me on her front lawn when I arrived.

"You know, you really should try and hide your identity as a dragon," she told me when I landed.

I transformed back to a Helmam and said to her. "I don't need to hide my identity as a dragon. Pretty much all of Housay knows that there are dragons living here. Soon, we will not have to worry anymore."

Sylfano looked at my hand. "What's that?"

"Oh, yeah," as I showed her my ring.

"Where did you get that?" She asked with wide eyes. "That's a dragon's ring!"

I smiled, "My real father made this for me," I said, "My mother just gave it to me today."

"Did she tell you what it does?"

"She told me that each dragon ring has a different affect for the wearer."

"Yeah. Well, that ring's symbol represents hidden strength, so it should increase your strength."

"I know! I felt stronger as soon as I put it on."

Haruasore's transport pulled into the driveway, and out came out Jamano and Haruasore.

"We are ready to leave," Jamano said.

"OK, so let's fly away then," Sylfano, said as she transformed into her dragon form.

"Wait! We're flying to the Ancient Kingdom of the Dragons?" Jamano asked. "I thought we will walk."

"First we fly to the Kingdom, but halfway there, we will have to walk. If gargoyles see that we are flying to the Kingdom they will attack us. Besides, there is no way for us to pass the borderlines without flying. I mean, you have seen the huge wall, right?"

"Yeah, I guess you're right," Jamano admitted.

Haruasore got on my back, while Jamano got on Sylfano, then we flew into the sky, not knowing that I was going to change the war in a way no one, except perhaps my birth father, would have expected.

The End

A Sneak Peek of Book 2

Chapter 1

Using My Senses

"Ok, Dracollus that's enough flying for the day," Sylfano said to me transpathically as she flew closer to the ground.

Sylfano and I had been flying for the past 10 hours with no rest. Ever since we all left Housay there haven't been any gargoyles trying to attack us. Sylfano landed on the ground. I landed right next to her. Jamano got off Sylfano's back, as Haruasore got off mine. I was a little tired from all that flying, but Sylfano looked exhausted. She looked like she could pass out any minute. Sylfano put the bags she was holding in her paws on the ground and transformed back into a Helmam. I transformed back into a Helmam as well.

"So what now?" I asked.

"Now, we set up camp," she replied.

She then took out a book from her traveling bag. The book title was 'The Survival Tent Book.' I rolled my eyes.

"Are you kidding me?" I snapped. "We need to set up camp and you need instructions on how to survive."

"This is no ordinary book. You should never judge a book by its cover. Watch."

She opened the book and put it on the ground. She then moved away from the book. Just then a tent had emerged from the book. I mean an actual tent like the ones you use for camping. The tent was big enough for two people to sleep in.

"Whoa!" Jamano and I said.

"Amazing it isn't?" Sylfano asked. "Come on in and have a look inside." She unzipped the tent entrance.

The fabric the tent was made from the outside was green, but the inside of the tent was blue. There were some images of dragons embedded in the fabric. There were two sleeping bags in the tent, but the place was big enough to hold four people.

"Who's going to be sleeping here?" I asked Sylfano as I exited the tent.

"Haruasore and Jamano will be sleeping here," she replied. "You will have a different tent."

"Where will you be sleeping?" Jamano asked her.

Sylfano smiled with a sad look in her eyes.

"I won't be sleeping tonight," she said.

"*What*?" We all exclaimed, including Haruasore.

"Why aren't you sleeping?" Haruasore said, "You look like you're about to pass out any second…"

9 781948 110068